ELIZABETH BEVARLY

THE BILLIONAIRE GETS HIS WAY

Published by Silhouette Books
America's Publisher of Contemporary Romance

 SILHOUETTE BOOKS

ISBN-13: 978-0-373-73078-0

Recycling programs
for this product may
not exist in your area.

THE BILLIONAIRE GETS HIS WAY

Copyright © 2011 by Elizabeth Bevarly

Books by Elizabeth Bevarly

ELIZABETH BEVARLY

is a *New York Times* bestselling, RITA® Award-nominated author of more than sixty books and novellas, and she recently celebrated the twentieth anniversary of seeing her first book in print—for Silhouette Books! Before writing, she worked in a variety of jobs, from retail to restaurant work to editorial assistant (never let anyone tell you a degree in English makes you unemployable), but now she happily makes her living writing full-time. She's lived in places as varied as San Juan, Puerto Rico and Haddonfield, New Jersey, but now makes her home in her native Kentucky with her husband and son and two cats of questionable sanity. (But then, aren't they all?)

One

All Violet Tandy had ever wanted out of life was a place to call home. A home of her own, not a foster home like the myriad ones where she grew up. The kind of home people had in old movies, with white clapboard and black shutters and full-grown sugar maples canopying the front yard. And a picket fence. Had to have a picket fence. And a broad front porch with a wicker swing where she could reread all the books she'd loved as a child—*Jane Eyre* and Judy Blume, *Lassie Come Home* and Louisa May Alcott. Only she'd *own* the books and not have to return them to the library every week.

Roses and lilac bushes would grow lush and fragrant around the perimeter of her house, morning glory would zigzag up the chimney and wisteria would drip from the eaves of the back porch. She would crochet wispy sweaters and bake cheerful pastries to support herself. She would live and let live and be content with her solitary existence.

And she would never, ever harm another living soul. Yep, a tranquil, unsullied life in a comfy, uncluttered cottage all to herself was the only thing Violet Tandy had ever wanted.

Which was why she wrote a memoir about being a high-priced, high-society call girl.

Not that Violet had ever actually been a call girl, high-priced, high-society or otherwise. And not that her memoir was actually a memoir—it was a novel written to read like one, a trend she had noticed was becoming more and more popular with readers these days, herself included. Gracie Ledbetter, her editor at Rockcastle Books, had been so swept away by the story, that when she called Violet to make an offer on the book, she had admitted that if she didn't know better, she would have thought Violet actually was a call girl, and that her *novel*—and that was how Gracie had said it, as if she were italicizing it—was actually a *novelization*—again with the italics—of her real life experiences.

In fact, now that Violet thought about it, Gracie continued to do that—speak of the *novel* in italics, as if she'd never quite been convinced that the book was complete fiction. Even now, a year after Violet had signed the contract on the completed manuscript and a few weeks after the book's debut, Gracie still asked things like, "Does the Princess Suite at the Chicago Ambassador Hotel really make you feel like a princess when you're lying on the bed staring up at the castle mural on the ceiling?"

Well, how would Violet know? The only reason she'd even seen the Princess Suite at the Ambassador was because she'd worked there as a housekeeper and had changed the sheets on the bed. Whenever she reminded Gracie of that, however, her editor would reply, "Oh, *riiight*. Of *cooourse*. You worked there as a *housekeeper*. Not as a…you know," in a way that wasn't quite as convincing as Violet would have liked.

And once, Gracie had asked if the croque monsieur with truffle sauce at Chez Alain really could fill up a person for three days as the review of the five-star restaurant had claimed.

Well, how would Violet know? The only reason she'd even tasted the croque monsieur with truffle sauce at Chez Alain was because she'd worked there as a hostess, and all the employees had had a bite or two of new dishes every time the menu changed. Whenever she reminded Gracie of that, however, her editor would reply, "Oh, *riiight.* Of *cooourse.* You worked there as a *hostess.* Not as a…you know," in a way that wasn't quite as convincing as Violet would have liked.

No matter. She was certain that the reason Gracie asked such questions was simply because she got so carried away by the—quite fictional—prose. With any luck, the reading public would react similarly, and the book would soar to the top of the *New York Times* bestseller list, something that would earn Violet enough money to buy the snug little Norman Rockwell house in the Chicago suburbs that she'd always dreamed about.

Her initial advance for the book had actually been rather modest, but thanks to the reaction Gracie's executive editor had had to the revisions on the manuscript, they'd bumped up its initial print run, changed the title to *High Heels and Champagne and Sex, Oh, My!* and convinced Violet to take a pen name that sounded a lot racier than her own: Raven French. Although Violet had been hesitant about that last, she'd conceded, and the combination had worked brilliantly. Its first week of sale, *High Heels* had debuted at number twenty-nine on the list and gone back for a second printing. Then it jumped another four places the following week. Now it was poised to enter the top fifteen and, having gone back to print for a third time, would doubtless climb higher still in the weeks to come.

Which was how Violet-Tandy-slash-Raven-French came to be sitting behind a table stacked with copies of her book at a packed bookstore on Michigan Avenue one sunny afternoon in October. And how she came to be staring into the most extraordinary pair of blue eyes she had ever seen that belonged to one of the most gorgeous men she had ever beheld. He was sitting in the back row and hadn't taken those blue eyes off her once since seating himself. And his scrutiny, although not exactly unwelcome since he was, in case she hadn't mentioned it, gorgeous, was beginning to make Violet feel a tad squirmy.

He was just so…intense. So…overwhelming. So…gorgeous. And God, so *big*. Even though he was sitting, he was head and shoulders taller than all of the women— taller than even the handful of men—who were present, and his shoulders completely eclipsed the chair back. His hair seemed even blacker than her own, but where she'd let hers grow past her shoulders, his was cut short by an expert's hand. And those eyes… Pale, nearly translucent blue, startling in their clarity and framed by sweeping, dark lashes. Although it was Saturday, he was dressed in a dark suit, something else that made him stand out from the otherwise laid-back crowd.

Even Violet-slash-Raven wore a casual outfit, picked out by the publicist Rockcastle Books had assigned to her. Marie had advised the fashion-challenged Violet on every aspect of her authorial self. Today, she wore a pair of black trousers and three-quarter-sleeve black top with a deep V neckline, coupled with more-strap-than-shoe stilettos. All were, of course, from the finest couturiers, since Violet Tandy…ah, she meant Raven French…needed to look like the wildly successful author she was supposed to be.

Of course, Violet couldn't afford the expensive labels Raven needed on the rather modest advance for her book. Fortunately, Marie had pointed her toward a boutique off Michigan Avenue that specialized in the short-term rental of haute couture and expensive jewelry for Chicago women who wanted to pretend they were members of the high society that was normally denied them.

For her outfit today, Violet…or, rather, Raven…had opted for clothes by Prada and shoes by Stuart Weitzman. To complement both, Marie had chosen a dazzling Ritani jewelry set—a pendant, earrings and bracelet fashioned of exquisite diamonds and amethysts that matched the eyes that had given Violet her nickname.

Her real name, regrettably, was Candy. Candy Tandy. It was only one of the indignities her mother had bestowed upon her before the final one of abandoning her at the age of three in a discount store with a note pinned to her Smurfette sweatshirt describing her as a problem child that no one would ever be able to love.

But that, along with everything else that had happened in the past twenty-nine years, was the past. These days, Violet thought only about the future. A future in her wisteria-laden house where she would take in strays of all kinds—canine, feline, equine, bovine, she didn't care. She might even become a foster parent herself someday. But only if she could guarantee that the children in her care would stay in her care and never be shuttled from one place to another, as she'd been. They'd be able to make friends who wouldn't be taken from them, the way hers had inevitably been, and they'd make emotional connections to other people that went beyond superficial, the way she'd never been able to do.

For some reason, that drew her attention back to the blue-eyed man in the back row. He was still staring at her. Intensely. Overwhelmingly. Gorgeously. He was in no way the kind of person Violet had expected would read her novel. In fact, he seemed more like the kind of person who might have shown up in the book as a character—perhaps one of her fictional heroine's many fictional clients. Each was an amalgam of men Violet had modeled after the clients and patrons of her former places of employment. Rich men. Successful men. Powerful men. Men who cared more about their images, their reputations and their status in both business and society than anything else—any*one* else.

Somehow she managed to tug her gaze free of the man in the back row and drive it across the other people who had come to hear her speak about her book before having their copies signed. Mostly female, these were her real readers. Women who were fascinated by the idea of sex for sale and by female protagonists who were in charge of their own sexuality. Who used their sexuality, the most powerful weapon they possessed, to get whatever they wanted. Who enjoyed no-strings-attached encounters with powerful men who paid exorbitant amounts of money to have women do things to them—and to do things to the women in return—that many would never even consider doing or having done to them during regular lovemaking with their usual partners.

Frankly, Violet wasn't sure she got that. Not that she was so worldly in her own encounters. Certainly she'd had boyfriends from the time she was old enough to want one, and she'd lost her virginity when she was a teenager. But she'd never quite understood the fascination with sex that most people had. The men with whom she'd been involved hadn't been all that special—or made her feel all that special. Which, she supposed, was why there hadn't been all that many. The way she saw it, sex was a normal physical need, like eating or sleeping or bathing. Except needed a lot less often.

A college-aged woman who worked for the bookstore announced it was time to begin, bringing Violet's attention to the matter at hand. Namely, the gorgeous, overwhelming man in the back row.

No! she immediately corrected herself. To the talk she was supposed to give to the gorgeous, overwhelming man in the back row.

No! she corrected herself again. To everyone who had come to buy her book today—she did a quick count, multiplying the number of seats across by the number of rows deep, adding another fifteen for the people standing and figured the total to be…carry the six, add the eight… around fifty-two—people who had come to buy her book today. Wow.

Ka-ching. She could smell the wisteria already.

She spoke for twenty minutes, having chosen as her topic the aforementioned philosophy of women in charge of their own sexuality and the appeal of having sex without the hindrance of emotion to muck things up. She followed up with the conundrum of how something so physical could even be tied to something so emotional—like love, of all things—in the first place.

She avoided talking about her own life experiences since, one, she was something of a private person in that regard and, two, she really didn't think anyone would be interested in her poor-poor-pitiful-me background. Instead, she focused on the motivation, goals and journey of Roxanne, her book's protagonist. She talked about how each of the men who became Roxanne's clients symbolized some aspect of the human condition, and how her heroine's submission to each represented another milestone in her personal growth.

Oh, God, she was good.

In fact, Violet…she meant Raven…had organized the book so that each chapter after the first—in which Roxanne was hired by a Chicago madam named Isabella, who herself personified society's obsession with using sex to promote consumerism—was subtitled by the name of one of the character's many clients. There was introverted Michael, who represented Roxanne's need to let go of her inhibitions. And uncompromising William who showed her how following the rules wasn't always a bad thing. Studious Nathaniel kindled her quest for knowledge, while carefree Jack helped her recognize her capacity to feel joy. And all of them—it went without saying—were lovers of Olympian caliber who gave Roxanne mind-blowing orgasms along the way.

The book culminated in the final chapter, Ethan. Ethan was the idealized notion of the perfect man, the one who fulfilled Roxanne in ways none of the others had managed alone, and who carried her to both sexual and emotional heights that… Well, that didn't exist, quite frankly. Talk about a work of fiction. Ethan was ultra-masculine in every way, but could still respect a woman for all her strengths, desires and independence.

Yeah, like that was ever gonna happen in real life.

After finishing with her talk, Violet-Raven opened the floor to questions, and a dozen hands shot up. Not from the man in the back, though, she noted, in spite of the fact that he continued to study her with even more intensity than before. In fact, his intensity seemed to have turned into something akin to anger, because those amazing blue eyes narrowed now when he looked at her, and that full, luscious mouth turned down at the corners. She had no idea why he would react in such a way to a talk she'd thought was pretty danged insightful, so she turned her attention to the woman sitting next to him, an owner of one of the hands in the air.

"You there," she said with a smile as she pointed to the

white-haired, apple-cheeked woman in her seventies or eighties.

The woman smiled as she stood, the sort of smile that made Violet feel warm and wistful inside, because she looked like the grandmother Violet had always fantasized about having when she was a child. Someone who would bake cookies and darn socks and say, "Oh, my stars," and wear sweaters with horse appliqués.

"Is it true," the woman said in a sweet, gentle voice, "that you're the one who invented the sexual position called the 'centerfold spread?'"

Oh, my stars, Violet thought, struggling to keep a straight face. Clearly the woman's years were so advanced that she'd confused Violet-Raven as the heroine of the book, not its author.

"Um, no," she said. "That wasn't me. It was my book's protagonist, Roxanne."

Nana's eyebrows knit in a sign of clear confusion. "But I thought you were Roxanne."

"No, ma'am," Violet told her. "I'm, uh, Raven."

"But didn't you write the book?"

"Yes, but—"

"And the book is a memoir about a call girl."

"Yes, but—"

"Then you're the one who invented the position."

"No, I—"

"What I'd like to know," a woman with dark hair who was hipping a baby interrupted, "is exactly how the crème de menthe thing works. Now, did you drink that before performing oral sex on your customers, or was it meant for external use only?"

Violet was vaguely horrified by the personal pronoun used in the question. She'd read about the crème de menthe thing in a magazine. She'd never actually tried it. Why did the young woman assume otherwise?

"Actually, I never—"

But before she could even complete her reply, another woman, this one a college-aged blonde with little black glasses, stood and said, "My boyfriend and I are going to be spending the summer in Italy. Could you talk more about that sex club Francesco took you to in Milan?"

Violet opened her mouth to reply to that, but not a single word emerged. She was beginning to sense a pattern here. Everyone who had asked a question thought *she* was her fictional character Roxanne. They didn't seem to realize the book was fiction. Even though the story read like a memoir, the blurb on the cover flap made clear the work was a *novel*. The reviews had all been in the fiction section of whatever periodical was doing the reviewing. Not to mention the fact that Roxanne's adventures were so over-the-top, no one could possibly believe they had actually happened to anyone.

Could they?

The sex club/Francesco query evidently reminded a lot of people of questions they wanted to ask, because in the scant moment of Violet's silence, the crowd erupted into what felt like hundreds of questions. Did Violet really have sex with Sebastian on the roller coaster at Knott's Berry Farm? What was her *real* reason for not doing that porno Kevin wanted her to do? Where did she purchase those crotchless panties with the whistle sewn on them that Terrence had liked so much?

On and on it went until the crowd bordered on chaotic. That was when the young woman from the bookstore stepped in and, in a very effective crowd control voice, indicated that the question-and-answer segment had now concluded, and Ms. French would be happy to sign her book, and would everyone please line up in an orderly fashion who wished to have their copy of *High Heels and Champagne and Sex, Oh, My!* autographed.

Not everyone who had attended the signing got in line, but many did. And although most of those wanted to chat with Violet for a few moments about the book, the bookstore clerk thankfully kept the line moving so that Violet was spared having to hear too many more questions about Roxanne's exploits being her own. By the time she signed the last available copy—and my, but the fragrance of the roses was mingling with the wisteria at the sight of the empty table—she was battling writer's cramp and on the verge of exhaustion.

Unfortunately, as she was capping her Sharpie and envisioning her return to her apartment to don her grubbiest jeans and T-shirt and pop in a DVD of *Casablanca,* someone slammed another copy of the book down on the table in front of her. Hard. Startled, Violet glanced up and found herself gazing into incredible, nearly translucent blue eyes. Blue eyes that had now traveled miles beyond intense, and kilometers beyond anger, to debark at fury central.

"Um, hello," she managed to say. "I, ah…I'm sorry. I didn't see you standing there."

The fact that she had overlooked him—as impossible as that seemed even to her—made him narrow his eyes even more angrily. But he said nothing, only shoved the book across the table toward her. Hard.

Somehow she tore her gaze away from his and forced it to the book, which, she told herself, should have way more importance to her anyway. But her attention fell instead on the hand that had splayed open atop it, obscuring the cover art of black patent stilettos, champagne effervescing in a slender flute and red lace panties and bra tossed carelessly between them. It was a large, masculine hand whose thumb, by its placement, seemed to caress the red lace of the lingerie. A very large and masculine hand, in spite of the elegantly wrought ring that wrapped its third finger, gold inlaid with onyx, that might or might not be a wedding band, since the hand happened to be his left one. But the hand didn't move from the book, making it impossible for Violet to sign it, so she looked at him again. He stared at her with unmistakable hostility, and her confusion mounted.

She tried to remember if she'd met him somewhere before and unwittingly done something to generate such a reaction. Had she accidentally botched his reservations at Chez Alain or overlooked a smudge in his bathtub at the Ambassador Hotel? Had she messed up the hem of his trousers when she'd been a seamstress at Essex Tailors or sent home the wrong cuff links from the tony men's shop where she'd been a salesclerk? Absolutely not, she immediately decided. Not only had she never made such mistakes at her previous jobs, but she would definitely remember eyes like those and a man like him.

Since he evidently didn't want his book signed, she asked, as politely as she could, "Did, um, did you have a question?"

For a moment, he said nothing, but his expression changed, easing up infinitesimally. He looked at Violet almost as if *he* were the one trying to remember if he'd ever met *her* before, and what he might have unwittingly done to her. Which she found laughable in the extreme, since a man like him never did anything unwittingly.

Finally, he dropped his gaze to the book and removed his hand from its cover so that he could flip it open. He turned to a page toward the back that he had marked with a strip of what looked like paisley silk ripped brutally from some unsuspecting garment. Then he shoved the book toward Violet and thrust his finger at the heading.

"Chapter twenty-eight," he said.

That was it. No question, no observation, just the number of the final chapter of the book, the one headed "Ethan." Which of all the male characters Violet had written about in *High Heels,* was the one her readers had responded to most. He was the one who was cited in all the reviews the book had received so far, the one who was whispered breathlessly about by talk show hosts who had hyped the book on TV. He was the culmination of all things strong, masculine, confident and rich. When he moved in his worlds of business and society, he was ruthless, arrogant and overbearing. Although his couplings with Roxanne had been earthy, powerful and raw, there had been a tenderness inside him that almost—almost—made her heroine fall head over heels in love.

Which was yet another example of how fictional the book was, and how Violet couldn't possibly have written it from personal experience. No way would she ever fall in love. She lacked the capacity for such an emotion. She'd learned before she was a teenager not to get too emotionally invested in anyone, because, inevitably, she would be separated from them somehow. Either she'd be moved to a new foster home, or her new friend would be. Sometimes it was the foster parents themselves she lost, either to illness or economics or caprice.

No way was she ever going to risk actually falling in love with someone.

"Yes?" Violet asked the man. "Did you have a question about chapter twenty-eight? About Ethan?"

"Not a question," he said. "A demand."

"What kind of—"

"I demand a retraction," he stated without letting her finish.

Okay, now Violet was really confused. "A retraction?"

she echoed. "What for? Why would I need to print a retraction? The book is—"

"Malicious, defamatory and untrue," he finished for her. "Especially chapter twenty-eight."

Well, of course the book was untrue, she thought indignantly. It was a *novel*. Duh. Why did people keep thinking it was an actual memoir? Violet must be a better writer than she'd realized. Still, the rest of his accusation was ridiculous. Novels couldn't be malicious or defamatory, thanks to that untrue business. So his demand for a retraction was likewise ridiculous.

Nevertheless, she hesitated before replying, not wanting to upset this guy any more by insulting his alleged intelligence. Carefully, she began, "I'm sorry if you didn't enjoy the book, Mr....?"

Instead of giving her his name, he glared at her some more and said, "My enjoyment of it—or lack thereof—is immaterial. However, I do know for a fact that chapter twenty-eight is libelous and demands a retraction. Just because you changed the man's name to Ethan—"

"Changed his name?" Violet echoed. "I didn't change anyone's name. I didn't have to. Ethan is a fabrication. The book is a—"

"You can't disguise a man's identity simply by changing his name, Ms. French," the man continued relentlessly, as if she hadn't spoken. "You described Ethan's coloring, his profession, his office, his home, his hobbies, his interests, his physique, his...technique... Everything. In precise, *correct*, detail." At this, he snatched up the scrap of silk with which he'd marked the page. "You even identified the manufacturer of his underwear."

Violet shook her head in mystification. She couldn't decide whether her interrogator was simply a little misguided or a raging loony. She turned to the bookstore clerk, hoping she'd take matters into hand now as she had with the overly enthusiastic crowd earlier. But the young woman was staring at the dark-haired man in openmouthed silence, evidently even more overwhelmed by him than Violet.

So Violet turned back to her, ah, reader, still not sure what to say. Maybe if she played along with him for a minute, disregarding, for now, whether the book was a work of fiction or nonfiction, she could talk him down from whatever ledge he was standing on.

Cautiously, she ventured, "Um, a lot of men wear paisley silk boxers, Mr...."

Still, he didn't give her the name she'd not-so-subtly requested. Instead, he shook the scrap of silk at her and replied, "Not imported from an exclusive, little-known shop in Alsace for whom this design is completely unique."

Oh, really? Violet thought. Well, she'd read about the place in *Esquire* magazine—guess it wasn't as little known as he realized—and how they employed their own weavers and designers, and probably even their own worms, so that their garments were each utterly luxurious and completely one-of-a-kind. And also outrageously expensive, which was why she'd written that Ethan wore them.

Violet sighed with resignation. "I don't know what you're trying to say. Ethan is a character in my novel. The story is fiction. Roxanne isn't real. Ethan isn't real. If I described him in a way that resembles someone who actually exists, I assure you it was nothing more than serendipity. There are a lot of men out there who work and play and live the way the characters in my book do."

"You and your publisher may be marketing the book as a novel, but there's no question in anyone's mind that the work is based—and in no way loosely—on your actual experiences as a call girl."

"What?" Violet exclaimed. "That's not true! I've never—"

"There's also no question in anyone's mind about Ethan. You've described the man so explicitly and perfectly that everyone in Chicago knows who he is."

Violet spared a moment to be proud of herself for writing such great prose that she'd brought a character to life— almost literally—for so many of her readers. Then she remembered that this guy had just accused her of being a prostitute, and she got mad all over again. Unfortunately, before she could express that outrage, her assailant spewed more of his own.

"And if you don't print a retraction to this…this…" He thumped the book contemptuously. "This piece of trash—"

"Hey!" Violet objected. "It's not trash! It got a starred review in *Publishers Weekly!*"

"—then I assure you that *Ethan* is going to sue you for every nickel you receive from its sales."

"It's fiction!" she said again. "No one can sue me for anything."

"Not only that, but *Ethan* will make certain you never make another nickel in your life, because he will sue you for so much money, your great-grandchildren will be paying his."

Okay, that did it. When people started threatening her nonexistent family, Violet *really* got mad. She stood with enough force to make the bookstore clerk squeak like a mouse. Then she straightened to her full five-foot-eight, which was made nearly six feet in the three-inch heels she was wearing. Then she leaned forward and crowded the man's space as much as she could, narrowing her eyes at him menacingly.

Even at that, however, Mr. Paisley Pants still towered over her. And he looked way more menacingly back at her.

"Oh, and what are you? Ethan's fictional lawyer?"

He slapped down a business card on the table beside the book, but Violet didn't bother to look at it. She didn't care who he was. She wasn't about to print a retraction for something that wasn't even real.

"No," the man said. "I'm not Ethan's lawyer. I'm Ethan. And I have never had to pay a woman—especially one like you, Ms. French—for sex."

Two

By the time Gavin Mason slammed the door of his Michigan Avenue office behind himself, his anger had diminished not at all. It hadn't helped that, barely halfway through the seven-block walk from the bookstore, the sky had opened up and dumped sheets of cold October rain on him. Thankfully, since it was Saturday, there was no one around to see him looking so disheveled. Or to see him hurl the copy of *High Heels and Champagne and Sex, Oh, My!* across the room with all his might. The hardcover slammed against the wall opposite with enough force to rattle a trio of framed degrees hanging there. Then it toppled onto a pair of hand-blown, and not inexpensive, vases when it fell onto the credenza beneath.

He'd hoped his walk—either to the bookstore or back—would purge some of the rage he'd been harboring for the past week, ever since catching wind of the gossip that had been circling in both professional and social circles of Chicago. And he'd hoped he might find satisfaction in meeting face to face with that…that…that lying, scheming harridan whose blistering potboiler was burning up the bestseller list faster than it was shooting his life down in flames. Seizing control of the situation was the way Gavin handled every situation. He always took matters into his own hands, and he didn't let go until he felt like it.

But neither the walk nor his confrontation with Raven French had dispelled even the smallest iota of his anger. In fact, seeing her at the book signing, looking so carefree and confident and beautiful—dammit—had only compounded his resentment. Who the hell did she think she was, bolstering herself through the defamation of others? How could she be benefiting financially and enjoying herself by destroying other people's lives?

By destroying *his* life?

As he folded himself into the big, leather executive chair behind his big, mahogany executive desk, Gavin noted a light flashing on his personal office line. He had two messages. Although he was fairly certain he already knew what they were about—since virtually every call he'd received on his personal line this week had been about the same thing—he punched the button to replay them anyway.

Beep. "Darling," a familiar voice greeted him. But where the voice, which belonged to a woman named Desiree, was usually scorching with sexual promise, on the recording it was cold enough to chill magma. "I suddenly find myself facing a dilemma about tonight. I can either attend the Bellamys' party with you, which would mean sipping champagne and nibbling foie gras and rubbing shoulders with Gold Coast glitterati, or I can babysit my sister's horrible twins and spend the evening being kicked in the shins, picking food from my hair and being called a poopyhead. Guess which one I'd rather do?"

Under normal circumstances, that would have been an easy one for Gavin. Considering the way his life had been the past week, however, he wasn't going to go out on any limbs. Sure enough, it was about then that the rest of Desiree's message kicked in, making things crystal clear. She started with a particularly ripe expletive, segued into a thinly veiled threat of a lawsuit because her health may have been compromised by his consorting with prostitutes, and ended with several suggestions about what he should do with a number of his body parts, at least ninety percent of which were anatomically impossible. That message was followed by another, this time from a woman named Marta, with whom he was supposed to attend a pretty major fundraiser the following Friday night. Suffice it to say that she was cancelling, too, but her reason for doing so made Desiree's tirade sound like a children's recital of Mother Goose rhymes.

Gavin debated briefly whether or not he should call both women to reassure Desiree that her health couldn't have possibly been compromised—well, not her physical health anyway—because he'd always practiced safe sex, and, oh, yeah, he'd never *been* with a prostitute, and to tell Marta that the thing she'd said about his family jewels had really been uncalled for. Then he decided that doing that would probably only exacerbate an already volatile situation.

He bit back another oath as he deleted both messages and tried not to think about what he'd become in Chicago thanks to everyone's assumption that he was chapter twenty-eight in a call girl's memoir. He was a mockery in society, a pariah among women and a joke at work—and it wasn't good for the CEO of his own import-export company to be a joke. Although each condition posed its own set of problems, it was that last, of course, that bothered Gavin the most. He'd never much cared about his social standing—unless it affected his ability to do business, and being a mockery certainly wasn't good for that. As for women, he wasn't picky and could always find more to replace the ones who disappeared.

At least, he had been able to do that before. Now that rumors were circulating that he'd been using the services of a prostitute, and now that he was being ridiculed at every opportunity, the normally teeming pool of willing women was emptying fast. And, hell, he hadn't even been using the services of a prostitute. Of course, now that the pool of willing women was emptying, he might very well be reduced to such a practice.

Irony, thy name is Raven French.

Not that there weren't a host of other names he could call her. Not that there weren't a host of other names he had already called her….

Gavin expelled a long, irritated breath. He grabbed his perfectly knotted necktie with both fists and wrestled out the perfect Windsor knot he'd completed effortlessly that morning. He shrugged off his jacket, unbuttoned the top three buttons of his shirt and the cuffs of his sleeves, and rolled the latter to his elbows.

Work. That was what he needed. To work and to sue the pants off Raven French. Not that that was what it took to get Raven French out of her pants. Hell, she'd do that for anyone. Provided the price was right.

Inescapably, his mind wandered to the book signing, and he was reminded of how surprised he'd been when he first saw her. He had expected her to be brash and harsh, both in looks and demeanor, with too much makeup and too stylized hair and a voice strained by too many cigarettes, too much drink and too many late nights working. But except for the clingy clothes and mile-high heels, she hadn't looked like a call girl at all. In fact, she'd looked kind of…pretty. Kind of…sweet. Kind of…wholesome. And her eyes. She'd had the most extraordinary eyes he'd ever seen. Not just the color, but the clarity. The expression. The…

Damn. There was no other word for it. The honesty. Raven French had honest eyes.

All a part of the act, he told himself. Like the wholesome, sweet prettiness. It made sense that a woman who looked like that would be able to make a killing as a hooker. There were plenty of men who would pay top dollar for a woman who looked like the homecoming queen when the lights were on and performed like the class bad girl when the lights were off. Not that Gavin was one of those men. He liked women who performed *and* looked like the class bad girl. Women who had big hair and full lips and enormous breasts spilling from their too-small confinement.

Women who were a lot like call girls, now that he thought about it. Hmm. Evidently, irony went by more than one name.

He pushed the thought away. In fact, he pushed all thoughts of Raven French away. For now. He'd thrown down the gauntlet along with his card at the bookstore. And if his intentions hadn't been made clear enough to Ms. French then, they'd become crystal clear on Monday when his attorney contacted her publisher. Really, Gavin hadn't needed to go to the book signing this afternoon. In fact, his legal department had cautioned him not to. But he hadn't been able to help himself. He'd wanted to look Raven French in the eye. He'd wanted to see his adversary up close. He'd wanted to make it personal.

Because it *was* personal. Which made the battle different from Gavin's usual conflicts, and his adversary different from his usual nemeses. What Raven French had done to him and his reputation was reprehensible and indefensible. It was bad enough that she'd painted him as a man who would flout both the law and morality—never mind that he'd done both of those things on more than one occasion; he'd never been *caught* doing them. But, worse, she'd revealed things about him that he'd never told anyone. That he'd never *intended* to tell anyone. How she knew those things about him when she'd never met him before was beyond him. But now everyone else knew them, too.

He pushed the thought away again. He'd come into the office to work, something guaranteed to take his mind off Raven French and her expletive-deleted book. And off her extraordinary eyes. And her surprisingly sweet smile. And the way her black hair had tossed back bits of silver under the lights of the bookstore....

By Monday afternoon, Violet's anger was still sizzling, in spite of the passage of nearly two days since I'm-not-Ethan's-lawyer-I'm-Ethan had slapped down his business card and whipped up her resentment. They were two days she'd spent trying to brush off his threat of a lawsuit as ludicrous and unfounded—which it was—and trying to brush him off as ridiculous and harmless—which he was not.

And that, she supposed, was the problem. Her editor Gracie had called Violet that very morning to tell her his attorneys had been in touch with the publisher's attorneys, and they'd made thinly veiled threats about the material presented in the final chapter of her book. They hadn't sent anything on paper—yet—or even in email—yet—but they'd made clear they were revving up for the possibility if Rockcastle didn't do something quickly to address the defamation and slander contained therein.

Clearly, even if Not-Ethan's lawsuit was frivolous, the man himself wasn't. Even if the outcome of any legal proceedings would leave Violet cleared of wrongdoing, he could still proceed with his threat to sue her and her publisher. At best, he could ensure she would have to endure legal expenses she couldn't afford—although her book was selling well, that was money she wouldn't collect until she received her first royalty statement next year, and until then, she had to subsist on her modest advance. Not to mention this was the sort of thing that could drag on for a very long time, something that could potentially drain everything she made anyway.

And at worst, Mr. Paisley Silk Shorts could conceivably find a judge who was sympathetic enough about his charges to put a halt to the presses and book promotion until the legal battle could be settled. And considering the capriciousness of the reading public—out of sight, out of mind and all that—such a freeze of sales could spell the death knell of her career just when it was starting to take off. What publisher was going to want to stay with a writer who landed herself in legal trouble the first time out of the gate?

Now, as she stood across the street from a steel-and-glass Michigan Avenue high-rise, Violet withdrew the business card from the pocket of her most recently rented designer duds—a crimson-colored Ellen Tracy suit over an ivory shell that, together, retailed for more than a family of five consumed in groceries for a month. Already the man was costing her money she hadn't planned—nor could afford—to spend by necessitating another visit to Talk of the Town for clothing rental. Had she shown up here wearing something of her own, she never could have convinced him she was the successful novelist she was struggling to be—with no help from him, *thankyouverymuch*. No, had she shown up in something of her own, the only thing she would have convinced him of was that she was struggling, period.

Gavin Mason, she read from the heavy vellum business card. That was I'm-Not-Ethan's name. The only other bit of information on the card had to do with something called GMT, Inc., followed by the posh Michigan Avenue address directly across the street. Evidently, Gavin Mason was somebody so important at the company that he didn't need to include his position or email address on his business card.

Gee, Violet was going to go out on a limb and bet that GMT didn't stand for Greenwich Mean Time in this case, and probably stood for Gavin Mason Something-that-starts-with-a-*T*. Training her gaze up, up, up the massive building—since the address on the card indicated GMT, Inc. was on the thirty-third floor—she flipped the scrap of paper back and forth and back again. Technologies? she wondered. Telecommunications? Transnational?

Trouble, she finally decided. Definitely with a capital *T*. And that rhymed with *P*. And that stood for—

"Pooh," she said softly under her breath, forcing her feet to move her in the direction of the crosswalk. Gavin Mason wasn't trouble. Not with *any* kind of case on the *T*. She'd faced worse problems than him in her life. No way would she let a man like that deter her from achieving her dreams. Let him try to charge the unchargeable and prove the unproveable. Hell, the publicity would only boost sales of her book even more.

Ka-ching.

Unless, you know, he did manage to tie her up in legalities indefinitely. Which, she supposed, was why she was currently crossing the street toward his office.

Okay, okay, she relented. So maybe Gavin Mason really was Trouble with a capital *T,* but it rhymed with *C,* and that stood for—

"Crap," she muttered under her breath as she reached his side of the street and her feet began to slow. "Crap, crap, crap, crap, crap."

She wadded up the business card and tossed it into a nearby trash can. *Take* that, *trouble/Trouble. Hmpf.* And she tried not to think about how, by hedging on the capitalization thing, she had just assigned Gavin Mason the distinction of double-trouble.

She took a deep, fortifying breath and exhaled it slowly. She could do this. She could go to Gavin Mason's office and speak civilly to him about this matter. He'd had two days to cool off, as had she, and now they could both be reasonable. She could explain to him how she'd come to write her novel, and make him understand that it was a work of fiction. By the end of their meeting, they'd doubtless both be laughing about it.

Okay, maybe not laughing, she amended as she entered the skyscraper that housed GMT, Inc. Because the building didn't lend itself to levity, and it reeked of serious big business. The steel and glass of the outside was replicated inside, then made even colder and more solemn by the addition of a black granite floor and fixtures. The elevators were stainless steel outside and more black inside, and Violet rode shoulder to shoulder with people dressed in more black and gray.

It dawned on her then, the appropriateness of Gavin Mason's name. Seriousness and stone. Like everything else here. The utter opposite of someone named Candy Tandy and then further nicknamed Violet. She suddenly felt even more out of place in her rented duds. Not because of the suit's chicness and expense this time, but because of its hue. She usually liked bright colors and wore them well. But in this environment, wearing red made her feel as if she were standing in the middle of the bullfighting ring, waving the cape to taunt the biggest, baddest of them all.

The offices of GMT, Inc. were in keeping with the rest of the building, but somehow seemed even more severe. A lone receptionist—another study in gray from her clothing to her hair—sat behind a big black desk, with big black letters identifying the company looming on the white wall behind her. The other walls were bare, Violet noted, and the waiting area held only a quartet of empty and uncomfortable-looking chairs. There was no reading material to peruse for anyone who might be waiting. No music to listen to. Not so much as a charcoal print to ponder. Clearly, Gavin Mason didn't concern himself with creature comforts.

Then she remembered his paisley silk boxers. Well, not for other people, anyway.

She'd been worried that showing up without an appointment might cause a problem, but seeing the place so empty reassured her. After speaking with her editor this morning, Violet had deliberately decided to come just after lunchtime, hoping to catch the man sated and slowed with a full belly and before he got too tied up for the rest of his day. She hadn't worried that he wouldn't be here. He was obviously the kind of man who took his work seriously enough to never leave it. Hell, Violet wouldn't have been surprised if he lived in the building, too. It suited him, all cold and impersonal as it was.

Now, now, she admonished herself. *Don't go in with that attitude. You're here to make things better, not worse.*

As if cued by the thought, the receptionist glanced up from her computer screen. She apologized for not seeing Violet right away in a voice that sounded in no way apologetic, then asked what she could do for her.

"Hello," Violet said in as chipper a voice as she could manage. "I was wondering if it might be possible to steal a few moments with Mr. Mason. Gavin Mason," she quickly clarified. As if that needed clarification.

Obviously, it didn't, since the moment she'd uttered the first *Mason,* the receptionist had started shaking her head.

"I'm afraid Mr. Mason has a very full schedule today. I'm sorry."

"I realize he's a busy man," Violet said, "and I promise not to take any more of his time than necessary. Truly, just a few minutes would be all I'd need."

The receptionist smiled mechanically, then dropped her gaze to the computer screen and pushed a few buttons on her keyboard. "Perhaps if you can tell me what this is about, I can make an appointment for you later in the week."

Which would mean Violet had spent money on her rental clothing for nothing and would have to spend more later in the week. Not to mention stew over Gavin Mason's threats for another few days.

"Today would be much better," she said firmly. "I mean, I'm here now, and—" she threw a meaningful look over her shoulder at the waiting area "—and no one else is, and, as I said, it won't take long."

"Mr. Mason has a very full schedule today," the receptionist repeated crisply. "Perhaps if you can tell me what this is about, I can fit you in—"

"Later in the week," Violet chorused with her, then added politely, "doesn't work for me, I'm afraid."

"Well, perhaps if you'd made an appointment…"

Violet tried again. "Maybe if you told Mr. Mason I'm here, he would—"

"Mr. Mason has a very full schedule today."

"He might—"

"Perhaps if you can tell me what this is about, I can fit you in later in the week."

There was no way Violet was going to tell this woman she was here because Gavin Mason suspected her of being a call girl who'd written about him in a memoir that was really a novel. But if the only way she was going to see the man was later in the week, then she'd have to settle for that.

"Fine," she said. "I'd like to make an appointment with Gavin Mason later in the week."

The receptionist smiled, this time with great satisfaction, lifting her perfectly manicured hands to the keyboard before her. "And your meeting is in regard to…?"

"Public relations," Violet said off the top of her head.

The receptionist narrowed her eyes. "Can you be more specific?"

"No."

She narrowed her eyes some more but didn't push the issue. Instead, she studied her computer screen for a moment and said, "Come back at four-fifty-five on Friday. He can see you for five minutes."

Violet gaped at that, but didn't object. How could she? She was the one who had said it would only take a few minutes. A foot in the door, she reminded herself. That was all she needed.

"Fine," she said through gritted teeth.

"Your name?"

She started to reply with her real name, then realized Gavin Mason wouldn't recognize it. "Raven French."

She might as well have yelled that the receptionist's hair was on fire, so massive was the woman's reaction. Her hands faltered on the keyboard, she bolted backward in her chair, and when she jerked up her head to look at Violet again, her eyes were wide with horror.

"Raven French," she echoed. With no small amount of melodrama, too, Violet couldn't help thinking. Honestly, the woman might as well have been summoning some kind of B-movie hell spawn.

"*Ye-es,*" Violet said cautiously.

Now it was the receptionist who gaped. But she didn't

say anything, either. Her gaze never leaving Violet's, she rose unsteadily from her chair and began to back away, bumping into the wall behind herself before flattening her palms against it and sidling to the right.

"Stay right there," she finally said, her voice going even more Norma Desmond than before. "I think maybe Mr. Mason has a moment right now."

And with that, the woman disappeared behind the wall. Violet heard the clatter of something tumbling over, followed by a thump and the crash of breaking glass, and a not-so-quietly muttered—nor in any way professional—oath. Then there was the quick rapping of knuckles on a door and an even less-quiet—and even less professional—screech of "Oh my God, Mr. Mason, that horrible woman is here to see you. Here. In your office. Can you imagine the nerve?"

The screeching was then replaced by another clatter and thump, only this time it sounded more like something being thrown than being dropped, and the oaths that followed were the likes of which Violet hadn't heard since accidentally downloading *Scarface* from Netflix one night instead of *Sense and Sensibility,* which she had been so certain was next in her queue.

Then, suddenly, there was silence. And somehow, that was even scarier than *Say hello to my little friend!*

The receptionist suddenly reappeared from behind the wall. After a few delicate *ahems,* she said, "Mr. Mason will see you now."

"Um, thank you," Violet said.

But she didn't feel particularly grateful. In fact, by the time she moved around the wall and saw the door to Gavin Mason's office, her insides were taut with anxiety. As demanding as she'd been to see him, she halted at the threshold, now reluctant to enter. Bending at the waist, she peeked inside, looking left, then right, then left again.

But the room was empty. It was also nowhere near as sterile as the rest of the building, filled with massive, dark wood furnishings scattered atop an immense Persian rug that was woven in rich, jewel-tone colors. The paintings on the walls, too, were colossal, brutally executed abstracts in colors that were even denser than the rug. Clearly whoever inhabited the office was as bold and dynamic and larger-than-life as his possessions, but he hadn't come to work yet. Thinking she must have approached the wrong door, Violet straightened and began to take a step in retreat.

Then, out of nowhere, a large, capable hand snaked out, wrapping large, capable fingers around her wrist and jerking her through the doorway. Before she could even squeak out an objection, the door slammed shut behind her. Automatically, she spun around, but her revolution was hindered by her trapped wrist, and, unaccustomed to her heels, she lost her footing and pitched forward.

Right into Gavin Mason.

Three

When Anna had told him Raven French was waiting outside to see him, Gavin had been even more furious than he'd been Saturday at her book signing. It was easy—and safe—to defame a man from a distance. But coming to his office like this violated the first primal rule in *The Man Handbook:* You never challenge a man on his own turf unless you want to get your ass kicked from here to Abu Dhabi.

"What the hell are you doing here?" he asked by way of a greeting. Doubtless that violated some rule in whatever handbook women used to get by in life—probably something with the word *chocolate* in its title—since their first rule would almost certainly dictate polite behavior. Which was all the more reason, Gavin rationalized, to be impolite.

To her credit, she didn't flinch. Even though he had adopted his most menacing corporate bigshot behavior. Even though he towered over her. Even when he deliberately moved forward to crowd her space even more—and was assailed by the fragrance of something surprisingly subtle and even more surprisingly sweet. On the contrary, she met his gaze levelly and smiled. A flimsy, uneasy smile to be sure, but a smile nonetheless.

Men three times her size—who had infinitely more strength and power than she possessed—had practically wet themselves when Gavin had been this intentionally scary. Raven French, however, smiled. Which just went to show how very badly she'd underestimated him.

"And hello to you, too, Mr. Mason," she said. But her voice wasn't nearly as steady as it had been on Saturday. When he'd invaded her turf.

He said nothing in response to her salutation, since he was still waiting for an answer to his question. Both simply gazed at each other in silence, as if neither was sure how to proceed next.

Interesting. On Saturday, there had been no hesitation between them, even though they'd been on display in front of a number of bookstore patrons, which should have inhibited their exchange. Now when it was only the two of them, alone, neither seemed to know what to say.

He still couldn't believe she'd come here. No one challenged him. Ever. *He* was the challenger in any situation, be it the boardroom or the bedroom. If Raven French had even an ounce of sense, she'd realize that. And she'd give him satisfaction immediately, in whatever form he demanded it, be it a retraction for her ridiculous book or—

Or something else.

A thought started to creep into his brain at that, one he really had no business entertaining, so he tamped it down. That was a form of satisfaction he neither wanted nor needed from her. Even if she did have long inky shafts of hair that made a man want to wind great handfuls of it around his fist. Even if she did have extraordinary violet eyes a man could find himself drowning in. Even if she did have a red, ripe mouth that made a man want to commit mayhem.

That wasn't why he was here. It wasn't why she was here, either. Why was she here, anyway?

"Was there something you wanted, Ms. French?"

Immediately, he cursed himself for being the one to give in to their standoff. Damn. How had that happened?

She smiled again, a little less sharply than before, and he knew she had noticed the same thing. Damn. Again.

"Yes," she said. "I was hoping you and I could discuss this matter more reasonably than we did on Saturday. You could start by releasing me and giving me a little breathing space."

"What's to discuss?" he asked. But he didn't release her. Or give her any space. "You wrote a steaming pile of garbage that included a thinly veiled chapter about me that painted me in a very bad—not to mention false—light. Your book has significantly damaged both my professional and personal lives. And unless you come clean publicly and admit you were lying through your teeth, you'll have to pay for it."

She inhaled a deep breath and released it slowly. Then she surprised him by admitting, "You're right. That chapter is a pack of lies. In fact, every chapter in that book is a pack of lies. I admit it. None of what I said about any of the men in that book is true."

Gavin arched his eyebrows at that. She was already giving up? Evidently, his reputation had preceded him. But then, it always did. Maybe she really did know what she was up against here.

Reluctantly, he loosened his grip on her wrist and released it. But he was only reluctant because that left her less vulnerable. It wasn't because he'd actually kind of liked holding her wrist. Well, okay, he'd kind of liked holding her wrist. But only because it gave him the upper hand, that was all.

"You're admitting you made it all up?" he asked suspiciously.

She nodded. "Every word."

Now Gavin's eyebrows arrowed downward. She was saying exactly what he wanted to hear. So why wasn't he enjoying this more? Oh, right. Because she hadn't agreed to make her confession public. "And you're willing to admit that publicly?" he asked.

She nodded readily. "I am."

"You'll inform both local and national media outlets? Tell everyone that nothing in the chapter entitled 'Ethan' is true?"

"I will."

Okay, *that* was what he'd wanted to hear. But he still didn't feel triumphant. Why was she giving up so easily? Why wasn't she fighting him?

More to the point, why was he so disappointed that she wasn't?

Still needing to hear her spell it out, he asked, "You'll admit, in public, on national television and in the press, that you deliberately defamed me in your book?"

Her gaze skittered away from his and she shifted her weight from one foot to the other. Then she crossed her arms over her midsection in a way that could only be called defensive. "Well, um, no," she hedged. "I won't do that."

Ah-ha. *That* was why he'd been feeling disappointed. Because that last admission was the one he'd really wanted her to make. And now she wasn't. He suddenly felt strangely happy that they were still sparring. What was that all about?

"You'll admit it's all a pack of lies," he said, "but you won't admit it's defamatory?"

She smiled at him, and his confusion compounded. Because her smile was self-satisfied and somehow became her, and there was nothing becoming about a self-satisfied woman. Women were only supposed to be satisfied by the men in their lives, regardless of the nature of that satisfaction. Women satisfying themselves was—

Well, okay, women satisfying themselves was actually pretty erotic, he had to admit. But only when that self-satisfaction was sexual in nature. Even if it was Raven French doing that, it would still be erotic. In fact, he thought as he homed in again on her ripe, red mouth, if it was Raven French doing it, it would be even more—

Annoying, he immediately, adamantly, interrupted his own wayward musing. Unfortunately, like all men, once a sexual thought began to unravel in his mind, there was absolutely no way to stop it, and the next thing he knew, he had an image imprinted at the forefront of his brain of Raven French lying stark naked in the middle of his bed, one hand covering her breast, the other between her legs, stroking herself with measured, leisurely caresses and looking as if she were about to come apart at the seams.

Damn. An image like that wasn't going to go away anytime soon. And he had a busy afternoon ahead of him.

"That's right," she said.

For a single maddening moment, Gavin thought she was agreeing with his belief that women shouldn't be satisfying themselves unless it was sexually. For another, even more maddening moment, he thought she was going to reach behind herself and lock the door, peel off every stitch of clothing, and gratify herself right there in his office in exactly the way he had imagined.

Then he remembered that she was the enemy, that she had defamed and libeled him and turned him into a laughingstock at both work and play, and he reminded himself that, even if she did do that whole erotic self-satisfying thing right there in his office, it would be really bad form for him to enjoy watching her.

Wait. What was the question?

Oh, yeah. She'd been admitting she had flagrantly lied about him, but that flagrantly lying hadn't defamed him.

"Why plead guilty to the first, but not the second?" he asked.

"Because my book *is* a pack of lies, but it is in no way defamatory." He opened his mouth to object, but she hurried on. "It's *fiction,* Mr. Mason. Fiction is, by definition, untrue, and therefore lies. Likewise, by being untrue, it cannot be defamatory."

He bit back a growl of irritation. "So we're back to that again, are we? Your *novel* that everyone knows isn't a novel at all, but a memoir about your sordid, tawdry life."

"We're back to that because that's what's true. Not the part about my life being sordid and tawdry," she rushed to clarify. "Since it's neither of those things and never has been. Well, not *too* sordid," she clarified further after a telling second. "And only a little bit tawdry. And only in the past, not now. And only if you define tawdry in the sense of shoddy and unsophisticated, not crude and gaudy. And if you define the sordidness more as callousness and unpleasantness and not poverty and squalor. Okay, maybe poverty wouldn't be so out of place, but I did *not* come from squalor. Nor do I live in squalor now."

She spoke so rapid-fire and with such a roundabout delivery that Gavin's brain was looped in knots by the time she finished—she *was* finished, wasn't she?—with her... whatever it was she'd been talking about.

"The book is fiction," she continued before he had a chance to think any more about what she'd said. Not that he wanted to think any more about it, since that would probably make his brain explode. "There's no way you can prove otherwise."

Due to the fog that had rolled in over his thinking, it took another moment for her statement to settle in. But when it did, just like that, the fogged cleared, and Gavin felt the upper hand slip back into his grasp. "I can't, can I?"

Something in his tone must have notched a chink in her determination, because her expression, which had begun to grow smug, suddenly went a bit slack. "Um, no?" she replied—in the inquisitive tense, not the demonstrative, which heartened him even more. "No, you can't?"

"Ms. French, I can not only argue that the book is nonfiction, I can prove it."

"That's impossible?" she said. Asked. Whatever. "Because there's no way to prove it? Because it's all a figment of my imagination?"

"Really?" Gavin said. Asked. Whatever. Dammit.

This time, Raven French only nodded her reply. Evidently she, too, had realized that she was beginning to sound like an uncertain second-grader.

He strode over to his desk and withdrew his copy of *High Heels and Champagne and Sex, Oh, My!* from the drawer into which he had crammed it over the weekend. As he thumbed through the pages, he made his way back to where Raven French was standing, this time stopping with even less space between them than before to make her even edgier. Immediately, she took a step in retreat. Without looking up, he completed another step forward. That elicited another one backward from Ms. So-called Raven French.

"Tell me," he said as he continued to flip through the pages and took yet another step forward, knowing it would be impossible for her to retreat further, since the door was now at her back. "Is Raven French your real name?"

When she didn't answer right away, Gavin glanced up from the book to see that she'd bowed her head and was fiddling with a button on the sleeve of her jacket. When he looked at her face, he was astonished to find that she was blushing. What kind of high-price call girl blushed?

Immediately, he answered himself, *Those whose prices are so high because they've become such accomplished actresses.*

Doubtless the blushing was a part of her professional persona. Or at least had been when she was making a living on her back—or her stomach or knees or whatever position commanded the most money—before she had begun to support herself with the more honorable profession of libel.

"Ms. French?" he prodded. "Raven? Is that your real name?"

"Um, no. It's a pen name."

Just as he'd suspected. "And why would you take a pen name, unless it was to protect yourself from all the men you'd be outing in your book and all the lawsuits that would result once it was published?"

Still not looking at him, but at least giving up on making the button do something it clearly did not want to do, she replied, "Actually, it was the publisher's idea for me to take a pen name, not mine."

He nodded, found the page he wanted, marked it with his finger, and studied not-Raven French again. "So they must have wanted to protect themselves from all the lawsuits that would result once your book was published."

She did look up at that, but the moment her gaze connected with his, it skittered away again. And, once more, pink blossomed on both cheeks. Amazing, Gavin thought.

He couldn't remember the last time he'd had a conversation with a woman who blushed. Even by design.

"Actually," she said again, "they didn't think my name was, um, exciting enough. They thought the book would do better if the author's name actually sounded like a call girl's name."

"In that case, you won't mind telling me your real name."

"I guess not…." But her voice trailed off without her doing it.

Gavin said nothing, only did his best to crowd her space some more in an effort to make her even more uncomfortable. And he told himself it was because he wanted to maintain the upper hand and not because he was hoping maybe she'd blush again….

Violet's breath hitched tighter in her chest when Gavin Mason inched another millimeter toward her, an action she wouldn't have thought possible since the guy had practically crawled inside her already. And dammit, she really wished her muddled brain had put that another way, because saying anything about him being inside her only made her thoughts even more muddled.

She tried to pretend his nearness had no effect on her. Because his nearness really did have no effect on her. None whatsoever. Not a bit. In fact, she had barely noticed how much warmer the air—among other things—became when he was this close. And she had hardly paid any attention to the scant spicy scent of him that teased her nose, or the way the lamplight in the room somehow made his arresting pale blue eyes even paler and more arresting. And no way had she paid any attention to his broad, broad, oh-my-God-they-were-like-a-football-field shoulders or his chiseled, honestly-he-could-slice-gouda-with-those-things cheekbones.

Nope, the only thing Violet noticed was how his nearness had no effect on her. In fact, she noticed that so much that she continued to gaze at the floor, because it was way more interesting than Gavin Mason.

"Ms....whatever your name is?" he prodded, making her twitch. "You were going to tell me your real name?"

Actually, she still hadn't decided whether she was going to do that or not. Even if she refused to tell him her real name, she was sure he'd find some way to discover it. Not that she was taking any great pains to hide it. It had been the publisher's idea, too, to copyright the book under her pen name. It wasn't unusual for authors who assumed pen names to do that, they'd told her. To protect their privacy, they'd said. In case they made a gazillion dollars with their books and became big celebrities, she'd been told.

Yeah, like that was going to happen with a big lawsuit hanging over her head.

"Violet," she heard herself say. Oh. Evidently part of her *had* made the decision to tell him her name. Would have been nice if that part of her had informed the other parts. "Violet Tandy." She started to go one step further and tell him that Violet was a nickname, and that her real name was Candy Tandy, but if he didn't believe Raven French was her real name, he certainly wasn't going to buy into Candy Tandy.

He had started to open the book again, but closed it once more. "Violet?" he asked, his voice reflecting his obvious bewilderment.

Something in his tone made her feel defensive for some reason, and she tipped her head back to look him defiantly in the eye. Doing that, however, only made her defiance crumble. Nevertheless, she squared her shoulders and commanded herself not to look away.

"Yes. Violet. Is there a problem with that?"

He opened his mouth to reply, then closed it again. Then he shook his head. "Not a problem. It just doesn't suit you, that's all."

Violet thought it suited her quite well, but she didn't want to make an issue of it, so she said nothing. Gavin must have thought she would, because he remained silent for a moment more, one dark eyebrow cocked in query. Strangely, he seemed a bit disappointed in her continued silence, but then he opened the book to the page he had marked.

And then—*oh, dammit*—he began to read aloud.

"The moment I saw Ethan, I knew he was a captain of industry, the kind of man who had built his business from the ground up. He'd begun with dirty fingernails and secondhand clothes, performing backbreaking labor from sunup 'til sundown to collect a paycheck that barely sustained him. He schooled himself at night, both in the ways of business and the streets, still managing to earn his degrees—yes, he had three of them—"

At this, he took a break from the reading to glance to the left. Violet followed his gaze and found herself looking at three framed degrees hanging on the wall.

"—three of them," Gavin continued, returning his attention to the book, "earning them in less time than his infinitely more privileged classmates took to earn one. And don't think the realization of that had humbled him in any way. On the contrary. Ethan's feelings of entitlement, authority and superiority were all rooted in those early days and had only flourished since.

"Those days were well in his past, however. When I met Ethan, he was wearing a twenty-five-hundred-dollar Canali suit—wool and cashmere, of course—and Santoni loafers that must have set him back at least another fifteen hundred. His tie, I knew, was a silk Hermès—I'd soon learn that all of his ties were silk, which made those evenings when he wanted to tie me to the bed with them that much more enjoyable—and his shirt was a fine cotton Ferragamo. I know my men's fashion, dear reader, and trust me. Ethan, more than any of the hundreds of men I've bedded, knew men's fashion, too."

He looked up from the page, closed the book, and stared straight at Violet. "I'm sorry I don't read out loud with the breathlessness and pretentiousness a passage like this demands, but—"

"Breathlessness?" Violet interrupted indignantly. *"Pretentiousness?"* she echoed even more angrily. "Roxanne isn't pretentious. Today's readers love all that name-dropping product placement. Didn't you ever watch *Sex and the City?* Jeez. And she's only breathless because her clients pay good money for that kind of thing. They want her to sound like Marilyn Monroe."

Gavin eyed her steadily, a faint smile dancing about his lips. "I thought you said this was fiction."

Violet felt her defensiveness rising to the fore again, and she straightened, squaring her shoulders once more. "It is fiction."

"The way you talk about Roxanne, she sounds like she's real."

Now Violet lifted her chin an indignant inch, too. "Well, she's real to me. All my characters feel real when I'm writing about them."

"Maybe because they *are* real? Real people you haven't even tried to disguise except for lamely changing their names?"

"No way," she stated adamantly. "You ask any novelist worth her salt, and she'll say she feels like her characters are real, even if she knows they aren't."

"Everything you wrote about Ethan in that passage could be said of me." He smiled in full now, but there wasn't anything happy in the gesture. "But then, you already know that. How you know it, I'm not sure, because much of it isn't common knowledge. You must have found someone who knew me twenty years ago in New York and paid them a bundle to reveal the information. Even more than I paid them to keep it quiet."

"I have no idea what you're talking about," Violet assured him. "I'd never heard of you before you forced your business card on me."

Now his smile turned indulgent. Which still wasn't happy. "Okay. Let's pretend you're as ignorant as you say. Let's act as if you really don't know anything about me."

"I *don't* know anything about—"

"You saw the letters on my card," he continued as if she hadn't spoken. "GMT stands for Gavin Mason TransAtlantic. I started off working as a longshoreman on the Brooklyn docks, loading and unloading ships for an auction house in Manhattan. Art, antiques, artifacts, that kind of thing. I didn't have much interest in what was in the crates I pulled off the ships. I just wanted to pay for the college classes I was taking at night. Until one of the auction house guys left a catalog behind one day and I saw how much some of that stuff was selling for. Six, seven figures, most of it. And the auction house got a nice bite of the take. Just for moving the pieces from one land mass to another and unloading it for the seller."

He smiled another one of those unhappy smiles. "Except that they weren't the ones unloading the items. I was. They got to stand in a climate controlled place and push around paper. I was the one lugging crates in the rain and snow. From sunup 'til sundown some days," he added, quoting the passage from the book. "And all I got was union wages. So I started taking more classes, in addition to studying for my business degree, to learn more about the import business.

And I still managed to graduate in less time than my...how did you put it?" He read from the book, even though Violet was sure he had the words memorized. "My infinitely more privileged classmates."

"But—"

"And those words *infinitely more privileged* are key here," he interrupted. "I'm a very important man in Chicago. No one here—no one—knows my background. As far as they're concerned, I was brought up in the same, infinitely more privileged, society they were. I've never gone to bed hungry. I've never lived in a crap apartment where the cockroaches and rats vied for crumbs. I've never had dirt under my fingernails, and I've never wondered which of a half dozen men might be my father."

Violet's back went up at his words, so full of contempt were they for a life of need. Except for the rats thing, he could have been talking about her own past. "And what's so terrible about all those things?" she demanded. "People can't help the circumstances they're born into. Poverty isn't a crime. I'd think you'd be proud of yourself for overcoming all those difficulties to become the man you are now." Then, although she had no idea why she would admit such a thing to him, she added, "I don't know who my father is, either."

"Yes, well, that doesn't exactly surprise me."

"Hey!"

He ignored her interjection. "I am proud of myself for overcoming my past," he said fiercely, "but that doesn't mean I want anyone else to know about it. The kind of people I rub shoulders with don't want to know poverty exists. They sure as hell don't want to know anyone personally who came from that world."

Well, that, Violet knew, was certainly true.

"They think I'm one of them," he continued. "That's a

big part of why I enjoy the kind of life I do now. I've worked hard not just to get to the top of my profession, but to get to the top of the social order, too. That's meant hiding the facts of my past from all of them. Which I've done very well." He held up the book. "Until now. Now everyone knows."

So it wasn't only the damage he thought his image had taken because people were saying he hired call girls that had him so up in arms, Violet thought. He was as angry—maybe even angrier—about people thinking he wasn't the pampered blueblood he presented himself to be.

Well, boo hoo hoo. There was nothing wrong with growing up needy. "Like I said, what's so terrible about that?"

"Breeding is everything with these people," he answered immediately. "It's not enough to be successful now. You have to come from the right mix of blood—the bluer, the better. Not from—" He halted abruptly. "Not from where I come from. And now, thanks to you, everyone knows where I come from."

"Well, I don't see how they can assume you're Ethan from that passage," she hedged. "I wrote that Ethan is a captain of industry. What you do isn't industrious. It's an import business."

"Industry, import," he repeated. "The two words are very similar. The same way the names Gavin and Ethan are."

"Similar sounding maybe, but they're not the same thing at all. The careers or the names."

"Still, you have to admit, now that you've heard about my circumstances, what you wrote about Ethan's background is almost identical to mine."

It wasn't identical. Sure, there were some similarities, but a lot of men in Gavin's position could have backgrounds similar to his. Many men like him—and women, for that matter—had started with nothing and built empires. To do that, of course, they would have had to do everything themselves and learn what they could and fight their way up the ladder. It was all the more proof that the character of Ethan was a blend of many people, someone she'd created after reading books and articles about dozens of self-made millionaires.

"There are a lot of people who built their businesses the way you did," she pointed out. "That passage doesn't prove anything. Besides, you said hardly anyone knows your history that far back. So why would you think anyone would draw the conclusion that you're Ethan based on that description?"

He said nothing in response to that, and Violet hoped maybe that would be the end of it. Then, without a word, he dropped a hand to the top button of his suit jacket and pushed it slowly through its hole. Then he unbuttoned the other one. As he walked toward Violet again, he began to shrug out of it, something that made a funny little sensation fizz in her belly. He draped the jacket over one arm and went for his necktie next, loosening the knot at his throat enough to unfasten the top two buttons of his shirt, as well.

For a moment, Violet thought he was undressing for… for…for *something*…something he really shouldn't be undressing for, not in his office, and not when she barely knew him, and not when she had already been having thoughts about him she absolutely, unequivocally should not be thinking. But he stopped when a good foot of space still lay between them, and when he reached for her, it wasn't to pull her close. It was to—

Offer her his jacket? But that was such a gentlemanly thing to do, she thought, confused. And he was no gentleman. Besides, it wasn't cold in the office. In fact, it seemed to be getting hotter and hotter with every passing minute.

She shook her head, not even trying to hide her puzzlement. "I don't understand."

Somehow, he seemed to know the wayward direction her thoughts had taken, because his smile was full of mischief. And wow, when he smiled like that, as if he meant it, he was really kind of…slightly…rather…

She bit back a sigh that came out of nowhere. Breathtaking. That's what he was when he smiled like that.

"The label, Ms. Tandy," he said. "Check the label in the jacket."

Her brain still a bit foggy—never mind some of her other body parts that had no business being foggy in mixed company—it took a moment for her to figure out what he meant. "Oh. Right. The label."

She took the garment from him and turned it until she found the designer's name stitched to the lining beneath the collar. "Canali," she read. Just like Ethan's.

"And what kind of fabric?"

She searched the jacket again, this time looking for the smaller label on the inside seam that would offer the information. "Wool and cashmere," she read. "But how do I know you didn't buy that after reading the book, just to make your ridiculous charge seem real?"

"I bought this suit two years ago for a professional portrait I had made. Two years ago," he added adamantly. "Check the shirt and tie, too," he instructed.

She did. Ferragamo and Hermès, respectively.

He toed off a loafer and scooted it toward her with his foot. Santoni. Damn him.

He opened the book again as he slipped his shoe on, flipped a few more pages, then began to read. "Ethan's work environment was a study in contradictions. The building that housed his office was a looming edifice of glass and metal, lacking in color or texture or character, as cold and stark and ruthless as the corporate world itself. But his office reflected the true magnificence, prosperity and hedonism of the man—rich colors, skillfully, beautifully wrought furnishings, decadent artwork."

Gavin paused there, looking up to meet Violet's gaze. Of course, she knew why. He wanted to gauge her reaction to what she knew came next. She had written the passage, after all. But she felt trapped somehow, pinned by his gaze, uncertain what she could say or do that would prevent him from reading the next paragraph. And when she said nothing to stop him, he seemed as if he were looking forward to reading the words that ensued.

"I have many, very special, memories of an oxblood leather chair tucked into one corner."

At this, he glanced at something over her right shoulder. Sensing what she would see, she turned around anyway, only to find—*ta da!*—an oxblood leather chair tucked into that corner of the room. Damn. That didn't look good. She turned back to Gavin, but he'd dropped his gaze to the book.

"So often," he read, "when Ethan requested I come to his office for one of our sessions, he would be sitting in that chair upon my arrival, a cut crystal tumbler of fine, single-malt Scotch—neat, of course—in one hand. Without even greeting me, he would demand that I take off every stitch of clothing, which, of course, I would do. Then he would beckon me over and offer me the glass. I was to fill my mouth first with the Scotch, long enough to warm it, then drop to my knees and fill my mouth with him. As much of him as I could, anyway. I spent entire afternoons on my knees in that office by that chair, first giving him oral pleasure and then bent over the cushion so he could take me from behind, again and again and…" He halted and looked up at Violet once more, smiling even more broadly. "Well, I think I've made my point, haven't I?"

Oh, yes! Yes! Yes! Yessss! Violet wanted to shout. "Um, I believe you've tried," she said instead. She cleared her throat indelicately and avoided his gaze. "However, you failed."

"Oh?"

She nodded. And avoided his gaze some more. "Your artwork is in no way decadent."

Now Gavin raised both dark brows in surprise. "Ms., ah, Tandy, have you looked closely at those paintings?"

"Why do I need to look closely?" she replied. "They're all abstracts. I don't care much for abstract art. I mean, not that I'm much of an art connoisseur in the first place. But I really don't like the kind of art where I can't even tell what it's supposed to be."

"No, I'm sure you're more inclined to view the images in the *Kama Sutra,* but indulge me. That one over there, for instance," he said, pointing to one on the other side that was executed in bold lacerations of purple and brown. "What does that remind you of?"

She cocked her head to one side as she viewed it from this distance. "A peanut butter and jelly sandwich," she finally said. Well, that was what it reminded her of. Hey, she'd told him she wasn't an art connoisseur. So sue her.

He laughed at that, a full, uninhibited laugh that rippled over her, making something in her belly tighten. Not in a bad way, but in a way that made her feel...

Um, never mind.

"Move closer," he told her. "Tell me what you see."

She sighed, growing tired of his efforts to find comparisons between himself and Ethan where there simply were none. But she did as he requested, completing the half-dozen steps necessary to put her within five feet of the painting. She looked at it, trying not to focus on the individual parts and instead considering the whole. She let her focus blur a little, and, sure enough, a figure began to emerge from the swirls of colors. Not a peanut butter and jelly sandwich, but a…a… Hmm. It did look sort of familiar. In fact, it looked like a…like a…

"Oh. My. God," she finally said. "That's a man's…a man's, um…"

"A man's um-physical attribute that makes him a man," Gavin finished for her.

Violet spun around, gaping at him. "And you have it hanging in your office? That is *so* crass."

He laughed again. "The artist is massively in demand in the art community," he said. "Her greatest inspiration was Georgia O'Keeffe, but she's taken that artist's, ah, proclivities, one step further."

"Yeah, I'll say," Violet agreed. Unable to help herself, she looked at the other paintings in the room. Sure enough, a theme began to develop. One picture depicted—quite graphically, once you got the gist of it—a woman's, um… that part of a woman that made her a woman. Another picture was of a woman's breasts. And a fourth painting was of all the subjects of the other pictures coming together in a way that, had they been a magazine cover, would have had them banned in every decent grocery store in the Midwest.

"I cannot believe you have pornography hanging on your office walls," she said.

Gavin covered the distance between them until he stood beside Violet, towering over her as he had before. "Where does a woman who makes her living performing sex acts get off impugning a woman who paints them, or a man who collects those paintings?"

Enough. She'd had enough of Gavin Mason and his stupid ideas about her and her book. Settling her hands on her hips, she said, "The description of everything in that passage could be a description of a thousand buildings, offices and men in this country. I'm tired of arguing with you. You want to sue me, Mr. Mason, go ahead. *You'll* be hearing from *my* attorneys this afternoon."

With that, and without allowing him time to regroup and attack again, Violet turned on her heel and fled.

Four

Gavin watched Raven…Violet…whoever she was…flee—yes, that was definitely fleeing she was doing—until he heard the outer office door slam shut behind her, clueless what to say to stop her. What was odd was that he actually did want to stop her. What was even odder was his reason for wanting to stop her. Not so that he could threaten her again, but because after the conversation they'd had, he was more curious about her than ever.

How could a woman of her occupation not recognize the subject matter of the paintings hanging in his office? And then, once he pointed out to her what the subject matter was, how could a woman of her occupation be so shocked? To the point of being uncomfortable? Even offended?

He told himself it was another example of how she had been able to make so much money as a call girl, since it took a lot of talent for a seasoned prostitute to convincingly play naive. Doubtless there were a lot of men out there who found it arousing to bed an innocent who had to be schooled in the ways of sex. Frankly, Gavin didn't see the attraction. He liked his women worldly and sophisticated and adventurous. Who had the time or inclination to seduce someone with no experience? Who actually paid money for someone to pretend that? Gavin would rather get right to the action. Foreplay was way overrated. Hell, if he *were* going to pay a woman to have sex, it would be so she would skip over all that touching and fondling and stroking and licking and…and…and…

Where was he?

Oh, right. Marveling at Raven's…he meant Violet's… reaction to his decadent paintings. Which also made him wonder about her art commentary that had made her sound so pedestrian. Any high-priced call girl worth her salt would make it a point to school herself in whatever interests her elite clientele had, and art would definitely be an interest of an elite clientele.

Just who the hell was Violet Tandy? Who was Raven French? They were the same woman, but they seemed to have little in common.

She was playing a part, he told himself again. She'd slipped into the role she always plays with wealthy, powerful men to get what she wanted: Money. Maybe she wasn't earning a paycheck from him at the moment—well, not the way she normally did—but she was definitely protecting her financial assets by ensuring he didn't sue her. Of course she would deal with him the way she dealt with all her customers, by pretending to be something she wasn't. In this case sweet, innocent and vulnerable.

Yeah, right. Gavin wasn't one of her customers. He wasn't paying her anything. On the contrary, he wanted a piece of her. Which maybe wasn't the most tactful way to put it, but was appropriate in this case. He would have satisfaction. He would have a piece of Violet Tandy. And he would have it soon.

Violet didn't stop fleeing until she was five blocks from the shiny metal building that held Gavin Mason's decadent office and paintings. And she only stopped then because she'd reached the shop where she had to return her outfit. Talk of the Town was a cozy boutique off Michigan Avenue that rented haute couture fashion and accessories to women who needed to rent high society. It was owned by a woman named Ava Brenner, who had been incredibly helpful to Violet every time she'd come by the shop.

Ava was helping another woman when Violet entered, and her assistant was ringing up a transaction for another customer, so Violet stole a few moments to catch her breath and gather her thoughts. Inescapably, her thoughts turned to Gavin Mason, something that did nothing to quell her ragged breathing.

What had happened in his office? One minute, she'd felt so in control of the situation, and the next, he'd snatched it right out of her hands. She'd felt like a small, helpless creature running for its life with the big, bad wolf right on her tail, his rabid, hot breath dampening the back of her neck, his big, hot paws stroking the length of her spine, his slick, hot tongue tasting her nape, and—

And goodness, it was hot in here. What did Ava keep the thermostat on, anyway?

Violet inhaled a slow, deep breath and closed her eyes, willing her thoughts to clear and her heart rate to slow. Think beautiful thoughts, she told herself. That was how she had always reacted to stressful situations when she was a child. Whenever she found herself in a new foster home, or when the other kids were mean to her, or when friends were moved to a new home where she would never see them again. Beautiful thoughts. The ocean had been a favorite, even though she'd never seen the ocean in person. She'd seen it on TV often enough. And she had a very vivid imagination.

In her mind's eye, the ocean appeared, blue, blue water lapping at a sparkling white beach. The crisp azure sky was cloudless above it, the white-hot sun tossing diamonds onto the water's surface. Oh, yes. Violet was feeling calmer already. Now she placed herself in the scene, sitting at the water's edge, the foamy surf licking her toes, making her smile. A gentle breeze drifted over her shoulders, lifting a few errant strands of hair from her forehead. Then, suddenly, it wasn't the breeze nudging aside her hair—it was a man's fingertips. Violet turned her head into his touch, then looked into his face, and saw the strongest, most handsome, most delicious, most—

She snapped her eyes open again, her pulse rate rocketing, her breathing shallow. Dammit, now Gavin Mason was even invading her beautiful thoughts. How dare he?

"Miss Tandy, back so soon?"

Ava's question returned Violet well and truly to the present, reminding her of the matter at hand. Ava really was a lovely woman, even if she did nothing to play up her attributes. Her dark blond hair was swept up in a French twist, and if she was wearing any makeup, Violet sure couldn't tell. Her wide smoky eyes were thickly lashed, but not from mascara, and her mouth bore only a trace of gloss. She was dressed in a dove-gray suit that was doubtless as high fashion as her wares, a simple pearl necklace and studs her only accessories.

"I hope there wasn't a problem with the suit," she added. Her voice was completely at odds with her outward elegance, sounding of dark nights in smoky lounges and whiskey on the rocks. "If so, it will be the work of but a moment to find something more appropriate."

Violet smiled back. She'd never heard anyone talk the way Ava talked. She wondered what the woman's story was, why she was renting out fine clothing to women who couldn't afford to buy it when she was obviously a product of high society herself. Normally, people like that didn't want people like Violet anywhere near them. They wanted to forget people like Violet even existed. Oh, they didn't mind writing checks to organizations or attending fancy fundraisers that helped people who couldn't help themselves—*giving back to the community,* they called it, as if they'd ever come out of that community to begin with—but they didn't want to soil their white gloves by actually coming into contact with anyone who needed help. Yet here was Ava, offering a means for such people to infiltrate society. Violet bet, if she asked, Ava would even be able to supply the white gloves.

"No, the suit was perfect," she assured her. "My, ah, meeting didn't last as long as I thought it would, that's all."

Ava clasped her hands together in front of herself in a way that reminded Violet of a school librarian. "I hope it went well."

"Um, yeah," Violet lied. "Yeah, it went really, really well."

"Excellent."

"I'll, uh, go change if that's okay."

"Of course," Ava told her. "If you'd like to step into changing room B, I'll have Lucy bring you your things."

That was another thing Violet liked about Talk of the Town. If your rental wasn't overnight, you could check your street clothes for the day, thereby saving yourself a trip home and back. That plus the posh atmosphere and the fact that

Ava had a way of making you feel like a million bucks, even when you were wearing your grubby blue jeans and hoodie and hiking boots, made Violet wish she could move into Talk of the Town and live here forever.

Unfortunately, since Ava would probably frown on that, she didn't even ask. She simply changed into her grubby blue jeans and hoodie and hiking boots when Lucy brought them in to her, retrieved her damage deposit from same, and made her way out. The minute she hit the street, she was back in her real life. Her real life that wasn't anywhere near as glamorous and refined as one small boutique off Michigan Avenue could make it feel.

Still, Violet's real life wasn't all that bad, and was certainly an improvement over the one she'd had as a child and young woman. Her Wicker Park apartment was in a recently reclaimed and renovated brownstone in a row of other reclaimed and renovated brownstones, and had tons of character. Like creaky floors and a noisy radiator and windows that stuck when the summer became too humid. And maybe there was no elevator, but, hey, climbing five flights of stairs every day was a lot cheaper than joining a gym. And so what if it only had one bedroom and teeny living area and a kitchen that was the size of an electron? She had a view of the city that was pretty breathtaking, and being on the top floor gave her roof access that had allowed her to make a patio of sorts up there with potted plants and everything.

Okay, okay, it wasn't the Ritz. It was still a million miles away from the cramped apartments she'd called home growing up—such as they were, since "home" had always been a fluid concept. Even more fluid than the concept of "family," which had never been cemented in the first place. If one of her foster parents got sick, or if the building where they were living was condemned, or if some court order said so, then, hey, so sorry, you have to move somewhere else. And you won't know anyone there. And once you do get to know them, they'll be taken away from you anyway, so don't start caring about them unless you want to get hurt.

After Violet turned eighteen and was no longer a ward of the state, her living arrangements had really deteriorated, because she'd been working low-paying jobs and trying to save money for that house in the 'burbs that she was *this close* to making a reality...provided Gavin Mason didn't swoop down and ruin everything.

And *dammit,* there he was in her thoughts again. Would the man never leave her alone? She wasn't even safe in her own home!

The days that followed Violet's ill-fated trip to Gavin's office only hammered home how unsafe she was from him, but for entirely different reasons. Thanks to the success of her Saturday book signing, Marie was able to land Violet a meeting with a features writer for the *Sun-Times,* along with a couple of appearances on local news shows the following week. It should have been a writer's dream come true, all that publicity for her novel, but every time Violet spoke with an interviewer, it became clear that the person assumed the novel she'd created out of her imagination was actually a not-so-fictionalized account of her own experiences working as a high-priced, high-society call girl. Question after question addressed not Violet's protagonist, but Violet herself. At best, there was a wink, wink, nudge, nudge banter involved. More often, though, there was less-than-subtle innuendo.

Like she even knew what position fourteen of the *Kama Sutra* was. And she'd never even met Hugh Hefner, let alone had his love child. And French tickler? Wasn't that a city in Indiana? Worst of all, however, were the questions about her character of Ethan, and whether or not it was true he was modeled after a certain Chicago business magnate who shall remain nameless, but who everyone seemed to know the identity of anyway. No matter how many times Violet denied any knowledge of anything nonfictional in the week that followed her confrontation with Gavin, she grew more and more worried that no one believed a word.

The whole thing was nuts. The whole world was nuts. And casting a pall over all of it had been the specter of Gavin Mason, and whether or not he planned to go forth with his lawsuit. If the questions her interviewers were asking were any indication, however… Well, suffice it to say that Violet had a bad feeling about, oh…everything.

Although he had been surprisingly quiet after she left his office Monday, she didn't kid herself that meant he was backing off. A man like him probably needed a little extra time to hone his weaponry and get all his peons in a row. There was no room for error with a guy like that. He was probably just ordering his minions to line up every legal precedent they could find.

By Friday night, all Violet wanted to do was hole up in her apartment with a bunch of old movies. As she always did when she locked the door behind herself, she found herself wishing she had a pet of some kind. A dog who would meet her at the door with happy yipping and dancing, or a cat who would wind around her legs and then hop into her lap. Something—some*one*—who made her feel important and necessary and who kept the loneliness at bay. But the building didn't allow animals of any kind—not even fish—so, like always, Violet had to be her own best friend.

She made her way to her tiny bedroom, furnished in *fin de siècle* Paris, right down to the white wrought-iron bed, cabbage rose bedspread and fringed lamp shade. Even though it wasn't quite dark, she changed into a pair of flannel pajamas spattered with cartoon sushi and pinned her hair loosely atop her head. Hey, she didn't have plans for the evening, other than to watch a William Powell double feature and eat lots of ice cream. Having the specter of Gavin Mason hovering over one all week did have that I-need-ice-cream-and-I-need-it-now effect on a girl.

Dammit, there he was *again*. When she should be thinking about what flavor ice cream to have for dinner and whether she should watch *The Thin Man* or *My Man Godfrey* first.

As she entered her kitchen, she shoved all thoughts of Gavin Mason out of her brain and focused on more important matters. Cherry Garcia or Chunky Monkey—*there* was a dilemma. But it was easily settled by plunking a scoop of each into a big bowl. Now that's what Violet called living the high life. Who needed Dolce & Gabbana when you had Ben & Jerry?

The opening credits for *My Man Godfrey* had just finished when there was a knock at Violet's front door. Which did more than startle her, since not only was she not expecting anyone, but only the most dedicated serial killer would brave five flights of stairs, indicating the one at the door must be truly intent on wreaking mayhem.

Oh, stop it, she told herself. It was probably a delivery for her downstairs neighbor.

A quick peek through the peephole, however, and Violet knew it wasn't a delivery. She also knew it wasn't a serial killer. More was the pity. Because she would have been infinitely more grateful for one of those instead of Gavin Mason, who was, in fact, standing on the other side of the door. What on earth was he doing here?

"Who is it?" she called through the door.

"You know exactly who it is," he replied. "You have a peephole."

"Through a peephole, everyone looks like a giant fish," she stalled. "So unless you're a giant fish, then I don't know who you are. And even if you are a giant fish, I still don't know you, because I don't know any giant fish."

She heard an exasperated sound from the other side followed by "Open the damned door."

Violet hooked the chain in its groove, then opened the door the four inches that would allow. "Why, Mr. Mason," she said when she saw him. "To what do I owe this honor?"

She was proud of herself for not sounding anywhere near as uneasy as she felt. Really, what *was* he doing here? In a tuxedo? Looking freshly showered and shaved, and smelling even better than he had the last time she saw him?

He studied her intently for a moment. "Actually, it's you who owes me," he said. "And I'm here to give you a chance to make good on the debt."

Oh, she didn't like the sound of that *at all*. "I beg your pardon?" she said. Mostly because she had no idea what else to say.

"I had a date for a fundraiser tonight," he said. "A woman named Marta who read your book, recognized me in Ethan, and who now refuses to speak to me."

"Gee, that's a shame," Violet said. "Not that you don't have a date for the evening," she hastened to clarify, "but that you date women who don't have enough brains to recognize the difference between fact and fiction."

He frowned at that, obviously wondering if that was a dig at him, too. Which, of course, it was. But he said nothing, evidently thinking that best. Good man.

"Sorry I can't help you out," she told him. "But I'm not a dating service."

He smiled at that. Well, okay, it was actually more like gritting his teeth. But she was going to give him the benefit of the doubt—unlike some Chicago business magnates she knew—and go for smile. "No, you're certainly not a *dating* service," he agreed. "But I'm not here because I want you to fix me up with someone. I'm here because *you* owe me."

It took a moment for his meaning to gel in Violet's muddy brain. "You want *me* to go to this thing with you?" she asked incredulously.

"No, I don't want that. But I don't have much choice. No other woman in town will be seen with me, thanks to you. And going to this thing alone would only illustrate that fact to everyone there."

"Well, sorry, but I already have plans for the evening," she said. "Maybe next time you could call first. Surely if you can figure out where I live, you can locate my phone number. Both are unlisted, after all."

She started to push the door closed, but his hand shot out, his palm flattening against it, and he pushed it effortlessly to its limit again. "I don't think you understand, Ms. Tandy," he said. "You seem to think you have a choice in the matter. Like me, you don't."

She turned her shoulder to the door and pushed as hard as she could. It didn't budge. She told herself it was because she couldn't get any traction on the hardwood floor wearing socks. But she didn't really believe herself. With a fretful sigh, she gave up and looked through the gap in the door again.

"You owe me," he said again. "And I'm not leaving until you pay up."

Oh, she *really* didn't like the sound of that. "Do you honestly think I'd open my door to you after you say something like that? Not every woman is as dumb as Marta, you know."

He narrowed his eyes. "I need an escort to the fundraiser tonight. I figure since it was your damned book that put me in this situation, and since that's how you used to make your living, you can help me out by going in Marta's place. It's the least you can do."

Actually, the least she could do was slam the door in his face, but she'd already tried that and failed. It wasn't her fault Marta had bailed on him. The woman obviously wasn't the sharpest knife in the drawer. Gavin should be grateful she *had* bailed on him. He'd made clear his disdain for Violet, so why would he even want her to fill in for the woman who'd dumped him? That made no sense.

As if he'd read her mind, he said, "I've called every woman I know. None of them will even take my calls. The ones who haven't read your damned book have heard enough gossip to know I'm in it, and none of them wants anything to do with me anymore. The only reason no one rescinded my invitation to the fundraiser tonight is because I'm one of their biggest donors. Money talks, even louder than gossip. Except among women who are easily slighted."

Something in his voice almost—*almost*—made Violet feel bad for him. Until she remembered he was threatening her with a lawsuit that could upend her entire life and destroy a dream future she was *that* close to turning into a reality.

"Can I come in?" he asked, sounding almost—*almost*—solicitous. "I have a proposition for you."

Oh, she bet he did. So much for solicitous. Solici*ting* was more like it. "Thanks, but no thanks. As I've said a billion times, I'm not now, nor have I ever been, a call girl. Or an escort, either. I'm not interested in your…proposition."

He had the decency to wince at that. "Maybe that was a bad word choice. It's not that kind of proposition. Look, let me come in for a few minutes to talk, all right? I think we can help each other out."

"Oh, I don't think—"

"Let me in, Violet. *Now.*"

Five

Something in his voice when he uttered his demand made all Violet's reserve puddle around her ankles like something she'd rather not think about puddling around her ankles. After only a small hesitation, she closed the door, released the chain then opened it again. Gavin pushed past her into her apartment, and it was he, not she, who closed the door. Then, for good measure, he placed himself between it and Violet, making it truly impossible to escape from him.

Not that she wanted to escape. *Escape* was such a desperate word, after all. And she wasn't desperate. She was merely a little concerned. Okay, a lot concerned. For some reason, though, her fear wasn't for her physical safety. It was for something else she didn't think it would be a good idea to consider too closely.

"Here's the situation," he said. "The event tonight is a very big deal, not just because—" He halted abruptly, looking Violet up and down, from her head to her toes. "What the hell are you wearing? Is that sushi?"

For the first time, it occurred to her how underdressed she was. Then she reminded herself that she was relaxing at home, making her attire perfectly acceptable. Gavin was the one whose outfit was out of place—he was grossly *over*dressed. Yeah. Put the burden on him, where it belonged.

"Well, it's not like I'm wearing *real* sushi," she replied indignantly. "And pajamas are perfectly in keeping with my plans for the evening. Which is to do nothing."

She hoped she punctuated that announcement adamantly enough that he would realize he was wasting his time with whatever his *proposition* was.

"Well, you're going to have to change. You can't wear that to the Steepletons' party."

She crossed her arms over her midsection, realizing for the first time that her pajamas were so big, the sleeves nearly covered her hands. "Problem solved then. I'm not going to the Steepletons' party. Thanks so much for stopping by."

She started to reach past him for the doorknob, but as he had done at his office that day, he snaked out a hand, circling his fingers firmly around her wrist. Deftly, before she even realized his intent, he switched their positions so that she was between him and the door. Only where she had kept her distance from him, he crowded into her space again, anchoring one big hand on the door by her forehead and arcing the other arm on the door above her head. She tried to shrink away but found herself effectively pinned to the spot without him even touching her. In spite of that, her breath caught in her chest, heat pooled in her belly, and something snaked down her spine that left a trail of heat in its wake.

"Like I said, this event tonight is a very big deal for me,

not only because it raises money for a cause I respect, and not only because I'm one of the biggest, if not *the* biggest, donors." He dipped his head lower to hers, his voice going steely and cool. "But even more important than that right now, if I don't show up or, worse, if I show up without a date, it's going to look like I'm not there because I'm hiding out. Or, worse, that I can't get a date."

She swallowed with some difficulty, then pointed out, "But you *can't* get a date." Quickly, she added, "Not that that's my fault, since my book is a work of complete fic—"

"So I need to be there with a date. Because showing up with a beautiful woman on my arm will prove there are still some people who don't believe a word of your damned book, and there are still beautiful women who are willing to be seen with me."

Color her shallow, but it took a moment for Violet to move past the word *beautiful*. He thought she was beautiful? In her sushi pajamas? Then she remembered that both times he'd seen her before this evening, she'd been arrayed in thousands of dollars' worth of gorgeous rented clothing and accessories and artfully applied cosmetics. All modesty aside, she supposed she did clean up rather well. Still, it was obvious that his *beautiful*—both times—had been for Raven French, not Violet Tandy.

Then she moved on to the rest of his statement and realized a number of problems with it. "Okay, first," she said, "you showing up with the author of the book isn't going to do anything to dispel the so-called rumors that people think you're a character in the book."

"I won't be showing up with Raven French," he said. "I'll be showing up with Violet Tandy."

Oh. So did that mean those *beautifuls* had been for her, after all? And why did that make something inside her go all warm and fizzy? Who cared what Gavin Mason thought of her? The guy was a Neanderthal when it came to women.

"You can't show up with Violet," she said. "Violet doesn't have anything to wear to a high society party."

"Why not?"

"Because Violet doesn't go to high society parties."

He nodded at that. "Right. Violet only attends private parties, doesn't she? I guess the attire for that would be a bit limited. In more ways than one."

Okay, that did it. No more Ms. Nice Guy. Splaying both hands open on his chest, Violet pushed Gavin with all her might. The action must have caught him by surprise, because he actually stumbled backward a step or two, looking at her in disbelief when he finally came to a halt.

"Oh, no, you don't," she said. Before he had a chance to trap her again, she strode defiantly into the middle of her living room to put more distance between them, then spun around to face him. "You are not going to stand here, in my home, and impugn my reputation."

He laughed at that. A deep, full-throated laugh that came from somewhere deep inside him, sounding rich and dark and, well, kind of sexy, truth be told. Violet had always loved hearing men laugh, because they so seldom did, most of them. And Gavin's laughter was in keeping with the man—confident, powerful and larger-than-life.

"*I* impugn your reputation?" he managed to say through his laughter. "Sweetheart, you've done a fine job of that all by yourself. This may come as a shock to you, considering the world you live and work in, but even in today's decadent society, women who take money in exchange for sex don't have a reputation to impugn. It doesn't matter if you *are* making money now with…a different body part. Once a prostitute, always a pros—"

"I am not a prostitute!" she shouted at the top of her

lungs, hoping, in hindsight, that her downstairs neighbor wasn't home. "You know, you're not helping your own cause here if you expect me to do you a favor."

"It isn't a favor," he said, completely unfazed by her outburst. "It's your chance to pay up on a debt you owe me."

"But—"

"Think of it this way," he interrupted her. Again. "If you go to this fundraiser with me tonight, being no more than Violet Tandy, writer—not that you need to tell anyone what you wrote—I might be inclined to reconsider my lawsuit."

Now Violet was the one to narrow her eyes. "You're saying if I go to this party with you tonight you'll forget about suing me?"

"I said I'd reconsider it."

"Meaning?"

"Meaning maybe I'll change my mind about pursuing it."

Violet dropped her hands to her hips, a deliberate attempt to look less as if she were on the defense and more as if she were on the offense. Even if she still felt plenty defensive and in no way offensive. "*Maybe* isn't good enough," she told him.

"All right then. Probably. I'll probably change my mind about pursuing it."

"That's no better than maybe."

"Of course it's better," he told her. "Probably means much more likely than maybe."

"But it's still not definitely."

"It's still better than maybe. And it's the best offer you're going to get. And, it's only good for—" he lifted an arm and pulled back the jacket and shirt sleeve to reveal an elegant gold watch beneath "—another sixty seconds." He dropped his hand to his side. "One minute, Violet. Make a decision.

Either go with me tonight and instill a feeling of gratitude in me that might make me rethink prosecuting you for libel, slander and defamation of character, or turn me down and know I'll go after you with both guns drawn."

Oh, like that was any kind of choice. Heads he won, tails he also won. There was no guarantee of anything in it for Violet.

Except for the opportunity to attend a swanky Gold Coast party, she thought, which she'd never done before and doubtless never would again. Except for the chance to rub shoulders with the cream of Chicago society. And maybe, you know, get some material for her new novel, which so happened to be about the cream of Chicago society— fictional society, natch, lest there be some confusion about that at some point—and which was barely half finished. And which her publisher was breathing down her neck to turn in so they could capitalize on the success of *High Heels and Champagne and Sex! Oh, My!,* striking while the iron was hot and all that. So maybe there was a little something in it to benefit Violet. Other than spending an evening with Gavin Mason.

No! Spending an evening with Gavin Mason wasn't a benefit. That would be a punishment. The burden she had to bear in order to get the good stuff. Which was not Gavin, lest there be some confusion about that, too. Which maybe there was, since Violet was getting more confused by the moment, but—

"Thirty seconds, Violet."

She mentally ransacked her wardrobe, coming up empty until she remembered a black dress she'd purchased second-hand for a graduation from high school party. That had been ten years—and okay, okay, ten pounds—ago. But it was a forgiving jersey knit with a simple cut that would stay in style forever.

"Fifteen seconds."

Coupled with a rhinestone bracelet and earrings that could pass for cubic zirconium, provided the lighting wasn't great, and a pair of slender heels she'd worn to the same graduation party, and maybe, just maybe—

"Five seconds, Violet. Four, three, two—"

"Okay," she said. "Okay. I'll go to the party with you. And you, in turn, are promising you'll probably change your mind about the lawsuit."

He said nothing for a moment, then smiled. But instead of saying he promised to do anything, he only echoed one word. "Probably."

It was the best she was going to get, she told herself. And it was at least a little bit better than what she'd had before. Because there was a chance now, however small, that Gavin would leave her alone after tonight, and she'd never have to see him again.

So why didn't that make her feel at least a little bit better? In fact, why did she kind of feel worse?

Sugar rush, she finally concluded. All that ice cream was creating one of those carb crashes. Yeah. That had to be it. No other explanation made any sense.

"When can you be ready?" Gavin asked.

Violet looked down at her sushi pajamas, then at Gavin's flawless tuxedo. Then she drove her gaze higher, to his face, marveling again at how exquisitely his features were arranged. Never, she thought. She could never be ready for a man like him.

"Fifteen minutes," she told him. "Give me fifteen minutes, and I'm good."

Fifteen minutes, Gavin echoed to himself as he watched Violet hesitate at the entry to the Steepletons' ballroom. Fifteen minutes, she'd said, and she was good. Good.

Unbelievable. Not only did she look way better than *good*—words like *radiant, luminous* and *stunning* came most readily to mind—but any other woman would have needed hours to put herself together so well.

The black dress was styled simply, even modestly, with a straight neckline that went from collarbone to collarbone in front and had a slight dip in back that revealed just enough skin to make a man want to see more. But it hugged her curves like a lover's caress, making it not very modest at all. She'd even managed to twist her hair up into something sleek and elegant that revealed the slender column of her nape, a creamy span of flesh that beckoned to a man's fingertips…and mouth.

Her jewelry was a puzzle, however. Gavin had bought enough diamonds for his companions over the years—though not, God forbid, a ring of any kind—to know whether a woman's gems were real or not. Violet's were not. He would have thought that among her clientele over the years, there would have been at least a few generous types who gave her a trinket or two for services rendered, even if they were paying good money for those services. In Gavin's experience, men who bought women liked to decorate them from time to time, if for no other reason than to remind them who was really in charge of the arrangement. Evidently, Violet's customers had never given her anything but her required fee, otherwise she would have been wearing the real thing. Maybe he should get her a little something for—

For what? he immediately asked himself. For helping him out tonight? Why should he feel grateful because she'd done an amazing job of looking incredibly beautiful in a matter of minutes? Hell, she was used to putting herself together quickly. A woman in her profession would naturally need to wind things up with a client quickly and make an elegant exit to ensure being hired for another night, even if the jerk didn't buy her something nice now and then. Violet had had a lot of practice looking this good in fifteen minutes.

She turned around to look at him, smiling a soft smile. And just like that, Gavin felt like someone had punched him in the gut. Because when she smiled that way, without artifice or inhibition, she went beyond beautiful. That naiveté was back, but with it was an innocence and purity that he would have thought impossible to fake. For the first time, he could see why men would pay money, and lots of it, to bed her. Because bedding Violet would make a man feel like he was her very first, that no man had come before him, that he would leave an indelible impression on her that would outstay any man who came after him.

Maybe that wasn't exactly a PC way of thinking these days, but there it was just the same. A lot of men were still attracted to the notion of virginity. And if that virgin happened to know a lot about sex and was an eager partner, all the better. No wonder Violet's memoir had so many chapters in it. God knew how many men had come before Gavin.

His thinking halted him in his tracks—literally, since he had been about to step forward to escort Violet into the room. How could he be thinking about how many men had come before him, unless he was thinking about becoming one of Violet's men?

He didn't have time to ponder that further, because her smile increased, revealing a small dimple on one cheek that was... Damn. The only word he could think to describe it was *enchanting,* even though that was a word he normally, manfully, avoided.

"After blackmailing me to come to this thing," she said, "are you going to stand in the hallway all night?"

Well, no. Not when there were other rooms he'd much

rather make use of. He'd been to the Steepletons' house many times since meeting Richard a decade ago, and he knew for a fact that they had eight bedrooms in their Lakeshore Drive mansion. Gavin even had intimate knowledge of two of them, since he'd made use of them with his date during every party he'd attended here. He had intimate knowledge of the Steepletons' master bathroom, too. And one of the coat closets. And their gazebo. And a window seat in the dining room behind a pair of heavy drapes.

Good times. Good times.

"After you," he said to Violet now.

He splayed his hand at the small of her back, the warmth of her skin seeping through the soft fabric and into his fingers. The dress was so clingy, it was almost as if he were touching bare skin, which naturally made him wonder if Violet was as silky and creamy under her dress as the rest of her seemed to be.

The moment he touched her, however, she surged forward and away from him, almost as if he'd been holding a hot poker. So Gavin stepped forward, too, this time barely stroking her back with the tips of his fingers. Even that scant brush of contact made her twitch, but she didn't pull away from him this time. He gave her a moment to get used to the connection, then he moved forward once more, until scarcely a breath of air was between them.

Lowering his head to her ear, he said, very softly, "Don't flinch when I touch you, Violet. And don't pull away. You're my date, which means we are intimately involved. Don't do anything that will make others doubt that, or I'll have to reconsider my offer."

"Your offer was only to reconsider in the first place," she replied without turning around, her voice as quiet as his. But she sounded a little breathless, which, for some reason, made Gavin feel a little breathless, too. "How can you reconsider a reconsideration?"

"You'll find out if you do a bad job convincing everyone here that you're crazy about me and that we're only here long enough to make an appearance, after which we'll be escaping to have sex for the rest of the night because you can't keep your hands off me."

Now she turned around to face him fully, splashes of pink blossoming on each cheek. The blush was back. The surprising, alluring, strangely erotic blush. Gavin managed to keep his breathing in check, but wasn't quite as successful controlling another part of himself—a part he'd as soon not be losing control of at the moment, since the cut of his jacket was such that it wouldn't hide his condition.

"Now wait just one minute," she whispered. "There was nothing in this deal that said I had to pretend we're sexually involved. I'm supposed to be your date."

Gavin smiled at that. "Sweetheart, it's a given that any woman who's dating me is also sleeping with me. I assumed you knew that, since it's the same thing you wrote about Ethan."

She opened her mouth to respond to that, evidently thought better of what she had intended to say, and snapped her lips shut. Pity. He'd started to have all kinds of good ideas for that open mouth. Of course, none of them had involved talking...

He urged her forward, this time wrapping his arm around her waist and pulling her close. Screw the courtesies. It wasn't like he'd ever been big on courtesies with other women. Why should Violet be any different? Especially since she wasn't the sort of woman who commanded courtesy to begin with.

Ah, dammit, where was the bar?

He found it immediately, tucked into the same corner of

the ballroom where the Steepletons always put it, and he steered Violet in that direction. Before he could even ask her what she wanted, she requested a glass of champagne from the bartender, who poured it with great flourish before handing it to her with a smile. She smiled and thanked him warmly, then lifted the glass to her lips for a sip before declaring it delicious and thanking the bartender again. When the man turned to Gavin, Gavin barked out an order for his favorite Scotch, taking it from the man's extended hand without acknowledgment and guiding Violet toward a small pocket of people on the other side of the room.

"You know, you were very rude back there," she said as they threaded their way through the crowd.

Gavin had no idea what she was talking about. "What? When?"

"The bartender," she said. "You didn't even thank him for your drink."

"Why would I thank a bartender for doing his job?"

"Because it's a nice gesture," she said. "Because it makes someone in that position feel appreciated."

"Who cares if he feels appreciated? He's a bartender. It's not like he's trying to cure cancer or bring peace to a war-torn country."

"No, but he made this party more enjoyable for you by fixing you a nice drink. Therefore, you should thank him."

How could she possibly care about the hired help? Gavin wondered. Who even noticed the hired help? They were invisible. Or would be, if she would stop carping on them.

"Come on," he said, striving to make the bartender invisible again. "There are some people over here who need to see you with me."

He wasn't sure, but he thought she growled under her

breath at that. Which, truth be told, he found kind of erotic. But then, there was little about Violet tonight that he didn't find erotic, so maybe that wasn't surprising.

"This won't take long," he told her. "Nod and look sexy for a few minutes, and then we can move on to another group. If everything goes smoothly, and you play your part well, then I can have you out of here and home before midnight. Just like Cinderella."

Six

Cinderella. Yeah, Violet might feel like Cinderella this evening. If she were attending this party with Prince Charming instead of a big toad. Honestly, how had Gavin ever gotten any dates in the first place? Or, more to the point, how had he managed to have more than one with any given woman? Violet didn't care how handsome or sexy or rich or sexy or powerful or sexy or hot or sexy or… or…or…

Where was she?

Oh, yeah. She didn't care how whatever or sexy Gavin was. If this was the way he acted with women—with anyone—she wouldn't have spent more than ten minutes with him. Unfortunately, if she had any hope of getting rid of him and his stupid lawsuit, she would have to tolerate him for the rest of the evening.

Then again, if she had to suffer in silence, she thought as she savored another sip of champagne, at least she was doing it in gorgeous surroundings. She couldn't believe this place. The Steepletons must be soiled to their undergarments with their filthy lucre. As she and Gavin had made the lengthy journey from the front door to the ballroom, she'd thought the house really did look like something out of a fairy tale, complete with gold-limned wainscoting, marble floors and centuries-old oil-on-canvas renditions of peerage at play.

The ballroom was even more magnificent. Its satiny hardwood floor was inlaid with an intricate pattern of darker wood, and a massive crystal chandelier hung from the center of a ceiling that looked like a Renaissance rendition of heaven, right down to the chubby cherubs peeking over the clouds. The walls on three sides were papered to look like luscious gardens, and the fourth was composed of arched, beveled windows that looked out onto a massive courtyard below. Violet had just enough time to look outside and see that it was as beautifully landscaped as the wallpaper gardens were, lit by torchieres and candles, since some of the partygoers had spilled out there to chat and smoke.

Then Gavin was dragging her toward the group of people whom he'd deemed it so necessary must see them together. She figured out why immediately, since three members of the group were drop-dead beautiful women, all of them sporting form-fitting dresses of eye-popping color and gemstones that Violet was reasonably certain were real—and she wasn't talking real cubic zirconium, either. She had thought Gavin would simply walk right up and insinuate himself into the conversation, so it took her by surprise when he stopped a good fifteen feet away from them, removed her champagne from her hand to place it alongside his drink on the tray of a passing waiter, then swept her into his arms and began to dance.

It took him by surprise, too, since she had no idea

how to dance, something that became obvious when she immediately brought her foot down on top of his—hard.

"Ouch," he muttered, halting at once. He glared at her. "Why the hell did you do that?"

"Well, I didn't mean to. You might have warned me that you wanted to dance."

"Half the people in the room are dancing. Why would you need a warning for that?"

She didn't want to tell him it was because she didn't know how to dance. She was suddenly embarrassed to be at a party like this, in a place like this, surrounded by people like this, and have no idea how to perform any of the customs that were a part of this world. She was already keenly aware of how much more stylish the other partygoers were, and she was confident none of them had stopped by Talk of the Town to rent a gown before coming. The way they smiled and chatted with each other, it was obvious they all knew each other—or at least knew *of* each other. Even their posture and the way they walked and sipped their drinks was different from the way normal people—people like Violet—performed such tasks.

She was so out of place here, in a house like this, with people like Gavin. This might be the sort of thing she wrote about in one of her books, but her fictional version was nothing compared to the real thing. At least, in her fictional version, her characters—people like her—found some way to feel at home and be a part of things. The reality...

"Violet?"

Gavin's voice brought that reality crashing on her like a ton of ill-fitting dresses and cheap rhinestone jewelry. She remembered then that he'd tried to dance with her, and she'd failed abysmally, and now he wanted a reason why.

"What do you need, sweetheart, an engraved invitation?"

She sighed softly. "No, but a few lessons would help."

Her admission seemed to take him by surprise. His dark eyebrows arrowed downward. "Are you telling me you don't know how to dance?"

"Not this kind of dancing. Not where your bodies have to touch."

He opened his mouth to say something, but no words emerged. Then, after a moment, he closed it again. Once more, he took her hand in his, but this time, he led her in the opposite direction from which they'd been traveling. He didn't stop until he'd led her into a small alcove off the ballroom that led to a broader passageway beyond. There, he stopped, dropping one hand to Violet's hip, holding the other up at his side at chest level.

When she did nothing but stare at him, he expelled an impatient sound, wiggled his fingers as if waving at her, and instructed, "Take my hand."

"What about all those people in the other room that you said need to see us together?" she asked, stalling.

"They'll be here all night. There's plenty of time." He settled his hand confidently at the center of her back, then swallowed her hand in his. Man, he had big hands. "Besides," he added as he pulled her closer, "I don't want them to see me with someone who doesn't even know how to dance."

Right. Of course not. Here she'd been thinking maybe he had actually taken pity on her and wanted her to feel more comfortable by showing her some of the high society ropes. Hah.

"Put your left hand on my shoulder."

She lifted her hand to do so, but hesitated before touching him. She was suddenly aware of how close they were standing, closer, even, than they'd been when he'd towered over her at his office. As had happened then, the air around them grew warmer, and the clean, spicy scent of him assailed her. She noted the lean, rugged line of his jaw and the finely honed cheekbones, the pale blue eyes fringed with jet lashes. As had happened then, her heart began to beat faster, and her thinking grew foggy, and the entire world seemed to shrink until it was only the two of them.

"Violet," he said, his voice dropping even lower than before. "Put your hand on my shoulder."

After another small hesitation, she gingerly curved her hand over his shoulder. The fabric of the jacket was fine and smooth beneath her palm, and she fancied she could feel the heat of his skin seeping through it. Of course, it was her imagination. The man would have to be very warm indeed for it to penetrate layers of clothing. Then again, she was feeling more than a little warm herself...

"Now, do what I do," he said. "Take one step forward."

She stepped forward, then belatedly realized he'd meant that *he* was going to take a step forward, and she should follow him by taking a step back. The result was that the two of them pressed together even more closely, something that made Violet fancy she could feel even more heat emanating from him, and from a lot more than just his shoulder. She was already getting ready to defend herself against what she knew would be his charge that she should have realized what he meant—once her mouth stopped being so dry at the heat and nearness of him, she meant—but instead, he chuckled and muttered a soft apology.

An apology. From Gavin Mason.

"Okay, look," he said, his voice gentling. "I'll tell you what I'm going to do, and you follow, all right?"

Okay, now this was just weird, Violet thought. What had happened to the prickly, demanding type-A blowhard who had brought her to the party? Had aliens swooped in when she wasn't looking and replaced him with a pod person from outer space? And why was she complaining, anyway? A pod person would be way better company than Gavin Mason.

"All right," she said. "I'll try."

He dipped his head forward in acknowledgement, something that brought his face closer to hers than ever. Violet willed herself not to flinch, knowing he would pull back in a second.

But he didn't. He kept his head dipped toward hers, almost until they were touching. "Now then," he began again. "I'll step forward…."

He did so slowly, giving her plenty of time to follow him. So Violet took a tentative step backward.

"Good," he said. "Now bring the other leg to join the first."

She mimicked his action, trying not to notice how the movement of their legs against each other generated a delicious friction she felt in a lot more places than her leg.

"Now I'll step to my left…"

Violet followed a little more confidently this time, moving her foot to her right.

"Now I'm going to step backward…"

Violet stepped forward at precisely the same time.

"And now I'll step right…"

Already anticipating the move, Violet moved—almost fluidly—to her left, then laughed lightly at her success.

Gavin laughed, too, just as softly. "Congratulations, Miss Tandy, you mastered the box step."

"Do it again," she said eagerly, delighted by her success. "Faster this time. But not too fast."

He grinned, then nodded. As he repeated the steps, this time moving a little faster, Violet watched their feet moving back, to the side, up and to the other side. As he continued, she paid more attention to the music, and realized Gavin was keeping time with the flowing, graceful notes of the string quartet playing in the other room. Little by little, she grew more comfortable, until the awkwardness fell away, and she was actually dancing. Okay, box-stepping. It was still dancing. Gavin had said so.

She knew it was silly to take such delight in such a simple accomplishment—all they were doing was moving around in a square—but delighted was how she felt just the same. When she finally felt confident enough to take her attention off their feet, she looked at Gavin and smiled.

"Thank you," she said simply.

He looked surprised at that. "For what?"

"For teaching me the box step, Mr. Mason," she said, reverting to the playful formality he'd used with her a moment ago. "It was a lovely thing for you to do."

"*Lovely?*" he echoed, still dancing her in a square. "That's not a word people usually attribute to the things I do."

"Then maybe you should teach more people to dance."

He opened his mouth at that, as if he weren't sure what to make of the comment, then gave a wry smile. But he said nothing, only widened their square with every new step he took, until he was dancing Violet out of the alcove and into the ballroom. The music segued into something a little faster, but Gavin never missed a step…and neither did Violet. She wasn't sure how she managed not to stumble or trip over her own feet. It must have been because she had a good partner. But throughout the remainder of the piece, she and Gavin moved as a couple from one end of the ballroom to the other.

She was having so much fun, she honestly forgot all about how she was supposed to be angry with Gavin for a million different reasons. Until he looked over her shoulder at something behind her and said, "Right. Forgot. We're here to make an impression, not dance the night away."

They were? Since when?

Then Gavin was spinning her around, and she saw the same group of people he'd started to approach earlier, including the vibrant trio of beautiful women—one blonde, one brunette, one redhead. All statuesque and curvy, and all having exceeded their genetic potential when it came to, ah, filling out the upper half of their attire. And then spilling out of the upper half of their attire.

Inescapably, Violet glanced down at her own dress. Even if it had been cut low enough for her to spill out of it, she wouldn't even have trickled. As Gavin danced her backward toward the group, she began to feel as if she were flying the wrong way into a flock of exotic birds like a fruit bat. A dumpy, colorless, mewling fruit bat. With bits of bruised, rotting apple matted in her fur. It was all she could do not to lift a hand to her hair to make sure it wasn't sticky.

As Gavin slowed their bodies and roped his arm around her waist to walk her the rest of the way toward the group, Violet noticed there were men among the pack, too, all as beautiful as their dates and no less splendidly attired, even if their colors were much more muted grays and blacks. Violet had assumed Gavin intended to infiltrate the group and spend interminable minutes talking to them, and she was dreading having to hold her own in such a crowd. But he only nodded at them en masse as he passed, addressing a few of them by name, and asked one of the men—the one whose hand was cupping the derriere of one of the women *very* affectionately—how his wife was doing with the new twins. Then, without even waiting for an answer, he ushered Violet to the bar in the corner of the room and asked for two more drinks to replace the ones he'd given to the waiter before they'd even had a chance to enjoy them.

"Aren't you going to introduce me to your friends?" she asked dryly as she glanced at the group which, she couldn't help noticing, was paying an awful lot of attention to them. Way more than one would think they'd give to a man who had pretty much dismissed them all.

Gavin handed her a slender flute of champagne, picked up his own tumbler of Scotch and then—Violet could scarcely believe her ears—thanked the bartender for both. "They don't deserve an introduction," he said. "Especially not to someone like you."

And just like that, the magical evening came crashing down around her. Of course he wasn't going to introduce her to anyone here. He thought she was a hooker.

He seemed to understand immediately what she was thinking, because he said, "No, Violet, I meant they don't deserve an introduction because they're not my friends. They're awful people. You're way above them."

Yeah, because they were awful people. Didn't take much to be above a man who would grope a woman while his wife was home taking care of infant twins. Even a hooker was above that.

"They saw me with you having a good time," he continued. "That's all that matters."

Sure. That was all that mattered. That Gavin had seemed to be having a good time with a woman he would take home and have sex with, thereby upholding his image as the successful man about town who was in no way the model for the client of a call girl in her memoir, because he would never have to pay a woman to have sex with him. And he had kept her far enough away from them that they hadn't been able to tell that her dress was a ten-year-old castoff and her jewelry was crap.

Yep, they were having a good time all right. How long before the clock struck twelve?

Seven

Gavin wasn't sure when the change had come over Violet, but by the time he brought her home—before midnight, as he had promised—she had become downright sullen. As he climbed the darkened stairs of her apartment building—this couldn't possibly be a safe place for a woman living alone, since…

Waitaminnit. This couldn't be a safe place for a woman living alone, since the neighborhood was barely marginal, and the building was barely lit. Why would a woman who must have made a mint working as a call girl live in a dump like this?

It was yet another question to add to the hundreds of others Gavin had been asking himself since his first meeting with Violet, many of which had been stirred up tonight. Not just the conundrum of her dress and jewelry, or how she'd treated the hired help. But how could she not know how to dance? That was a major requirement for a woman like her. Call girls didn't make *all* their money in the bedroom. When a man was past his prime, for instance, and couldn't attract the sort of woman he really wanted, he often hired one to accompany him to events so people would think he was still a sexual stallion. And, okay, to have sex with the woman after the event, even if he performed more like a pony at that point.

Anyway, Gavin would have thought a high-priced call girl would be an expert at the tango, never mind at least knowing the box step. How had Violet ever managed to support herself, let alone have enough fodder for a memoir, if she couldn't even dance?

"Here we are," she said now, dispelling his thoughts. "Thanks for seeing me home." When Gavin said nothing in reply, she added pointedly, "Goodbye."

Translation: *Beat it.*

There was absolutely no reason for him to hang around. Even if some misplaced sense of chivalry had made him walk her to her door to be sure she made it safely—especially since it went without saying that a woman like her could more than take care of herself—he'd completed the task. He really should beat it. So why did he suddenly want to hang around?

"Aren't you going to invite me in for a nightcap?"

She hesitated a moment, though whether it was because his question had caught her off guard, or because she was actually considering an invitation, he couldn't say. "You shouldn't drink and drive," she told him.

"I had a drink at the party," he reminded her.

"Exactly my point," she replied quickly. "You've already had one drink tonight, even if you took your time with that one and had food to go with it. If you have another one, it could go straight to your head."

"You could feed me," he said. "And I could take my time with this one, too."

Once again, she hesitated before speaking, but again, he wasn't sure if it was because she was surprised by his wanting to spend time with her—not that he wasn't plenty surprised by that himself—or because she was mentally reviewing her pantry and wine rack to see if she had the proper supplies for entertaining.

Finally, tightly, she said, "Thank you for the evening, Gavin. Even though you didn't give me much time to prepare for it, and even though you pretty much blackmailed me into going out with you."

Oh, yeah. He'd forgotten about that. Maybe that was why she wasn't inviting him in.

"Now that I've upheld my end of the deal," she added, "it's time for you to do the same. Go home and reconsider your lawsuit. Go home and *probably* change your mind."

Right. That was what he had told her he would do, wasn't it? In spite of that, the last thing he wanted to think about at the moment was the lawsuit he planned to wage against Raven French. Which was beyond strange, because he'd barely been able to think about anything else for the past two weeks.

"I'll wait here until you get inside," he said, stalling. "You never know what kind of creep might be waiting for you on the other side of your door."

"Yeah, tell me about it," she muttered.

He wasn't positive, but he was pretty sure she'd had someone particular in mind when she said that. In a word, him.

"Go ahead," he said. "I'm not in any hurry."

She expelled an impatient sound, but opened her purse and withdrew her keys and started to unlock the front door. But Gavin intercepted her—again with the misplaced chivalry—and deftly took the keys from her hand, unlocking and opening the door himself. Before she could object, he strode past her inside, even though she had left a couple of lights on before leaving and there was obviously no one skulking about in the shadows.

"Oh, good, no creeps," she said as she followed him inside.

For some reason, the comment made Gavin feel a lot better about himself.

She pulled the door open wider behind herself. "Now you can go home with a clear conscience. Which will come in handy while you *probably* change your mind about suing me."

He really did wish she would quit carping on that.

"Good *night,* Gavin."

Conceding defeat, he retraced his steps until he stood framed by the door beside her. When she lifted her hand and turned it palm up, he obediently dropped her keys into it. Then he watched her fingers close over them, wondering at the spiral of disappointment that wound through him when she did.

"Thank you for coming with me tonight," he told her. "I know I didn't give you much choice, but…" He lifted one shoulder and let it drop, then repeated simply, "Thank you."

She met his gaze levelly for a moment, saying nothing, and in that moment, Gavin noted a tiny scar high on her cheek that he hadn't noticed before. It should have marred the flawlessness of her beauty, but somehow, it only made her that much more stunning. Even something that should have been a defect couldn't detract from the perfection of her features.

Before he realized what he was doing, he was tracing

the pad of his thumb over the blemish and asking, "What happened here?"

Her eyes went wide in panic, and her hand shot up to cover his and move it back down to his side. Then she placed her own hand completely over her cheek, as if wanting to hide the scar that was barely even noticeable. "Nothing major," she said, sounding a little breathless. "When I was eight, one of my sisters and I were doing the dishes. She was washing, I was drying. She dropped a glass as she was handing it to me, and it shattered on the counter. A piece of glass flew up and cut me. It probably could have gotten a stitch or two, but—" she halted abruptly, then quickly finished "—but it didn't."

It hadn't occurred to Gavin before now that Violet might have a family somewhere. Parents and siblings and all the baggage that came with them. She'd said *one of my sisters,* so she obviously had more than one. What had happened to estrange her from her family? Because, surely, she must be estranged. Women didn't become call girls if they had close ties to their families. Did they?

"How many sisters do you have?" Gavin asked.

She did the wide-eyed thing again, then dropped her gaze and busied herself with something in her purse. "Well, none, actually. Not biologically."

"But—"

"Look, it's late," she said, glancing up again. "You really should be going."

No need to tell me twice, Gavin thought. Even if, you know, she'd already told him twice. Maybe even three times.

He suddenly felt awkward for some reason, like a teenager bringing the girl he liked home from their first date. Unsure what to say, he finally stammered, "Well. Good night then. Violet. And thanks. Again."

He cursed himself for sounding like an idiot and started to turn away. Then, again without thinking, he found himself leaning down and brushing his lips lightly across the scar on her cheek. He had no idea what made him do it. Not only were they supposed to still be adversaries—in spite of the relatively peaceful way they'd spent the evening—but he'd never kissed a woman on the cheek in his life. Even on the playground in fifth grade, when he'd swooped in on Mary Jane Pulaski for the first kiss of his life, he'd aimed for her mouth. So what if he'd missed and kissed her ear? The point was that he'd been aiming for her mouth. And he hadn't kissed her cheek.

Violet gasped as his lips skimmed over her warm flesh, but she didn't push him away the way Mary Jane Pulaski had. She didn't throw a dirt clod at him the way Mary Jane had, either, which was a nice bonus. She did, however, splay her hand open over the center of his chest in a manner that said, *Don't,* and when Gavin pulled back to gaze at her face, he saw that she was blushing. Again.

He had no idea why he did what he did next. Maybe it was sparked by the challenge presented in her hand on his chest, or maybe he was driven by something else he shouldn't think too much about. But he lowered his head to hers again, this time aiming for—and capturing—her mouth, and this time he did a lot more than brush his lips lightly over hers.

He held his breath as he kissed her, waiting to see what she would do, something else he'd never done before. Never had he been uncertain when kissing a woman. Never had he doubted how she would react. It was that doubt, he thought, that made the kiss feel like more than it should. That could be the only reason why a shudder of heat shook him upon contact, why every nerve in his body surged to life, why the earth beneath his feet began to spin.

Why he felt like a kid kissing a girl for the very first time.

It was that realization, and not any resistance on Violet's part, that made Gavin pull away. But when he looked at her and saw how her eyes had closed and the way her lips were still parted, as if she expected him to continue, he immediately covered her mouth with his again. And this time...

This time, nothing else mattered at all.

Vaguely, he noted how the fingers that had been splayed open against his chest curled into the fabric of his shirt and clutched it tight. He registered the warmth of her mouth against his, welcoming him, rubbing lightly against his own. He felt the swell of her hips beneath his palms and knew he must have moved his hands there. She was so soft—all of her—so soft. So warm. So supple. He had never taken the time to notice before how erotic it could be to simply trace a woman's curves, how electric it could be to savor a woman's mouth against his own. So many firsts tonight. All because of Violet.

When he moved his hand up to cradle her breast in the deep V of his thumb and index finger, she gasped again. This time, when she opened her hand over his chest she did push him away. Then she took a step backward. Then another. And another. Her eyes wide with confusion, she pressed the back of her hand to her mouth, as if that might negate what had happened.

"Why did you do that?" she asked, her voice scarcely above a whisper.

All Gavin could do was shake his head. Not just because he didn't know the answer to that question, but because a million other questions were ricocheting through his head. And he didn't know the answer to any of those, either.

She moved her hand to her hair—he was astonished to

see that her fingers were trembling—and tucked behind her ear a long strand that had come free from the graceful twist. Had he done that? He couldn't remember. Then she crossed her hands tightly over her chest in a way he could only liken to defensive.

"You have to go," she said again, her voice as shaky as her hand had been. "Now. You have to go *now,* Gavin."

He had no idea what made him say the thing he said next. The words simply came out before he could stop them. "You're not a call girl, are you?"

He hadn't consciously planned to say that, but once the words were spoken, he knew they were true. Some part of him must have known the truth, and probably had for some time now. What else could explain this apartment, her plain dress and jewelry, her lack of knowledge about art and dancing…the way she had kissed him, as if it were the first time for her, too?

Not that Gavin thought she was that innocent. But he knew she wasn't that experienced, either.

"You're not, are you?" he asked again.

Now Violet was the one to shake her head. Her expression changed from one of confusion to something akin to relief. "Of course not," she said softly. "That's what I've been telling you since the beginning."

"But how…what…why…" Again, the questions bounced around in his brain, too many for him to articulate even one.

"I am mystified as to why everyone seems to think I wrote *High Heels* from experience."

That comment, at least, Gavin knew how to reply to. "It's that old saying, 'Write what you know.' That and the fact that you do write very, very well."

She braved a small smile at that. "Thanks. But you know,

if writers only wrote what they know, the world would be full of boring books. We can't all be Ernest Hemingway."

Well, no, Violet certainly wasn't him. Something for which Gavin was profoundly grateful at the moment. In fact, there were a lot of things he was grateful for at the moment. But he didn't want to think too much about any of them right now. In fact, all he wanted to do right now was kiss Violet again. So he covered what little distance she'd put between them and did just that.

Violet wasn't sure when the moment went from one of understanding to one of overwhelming. She only knew that in one instant, Gavin had finally accepted the truth about her and the next…

Oh, the next. The next she was feeling something she'd felt for a few brief moments earlier in the evening, when Gavin was teaching her to dance. Something she'd never felt before, only now she was feeling it a million times more strongly. It was the kind of thing that made a person feel…close…to another person. The kind of thing she had been certain she wasn't wired to feel. Feeling it again now, like this, it was as if a door had opened up inside her and let loose something that had been held captive for too long. She wanted to keep feeling it, wanted to see how fast and how far it would go.

But as he captured her mouth with his more urgently, as his fingers curled more insistently over her hips, her thoughts evaporated. It had been so long since a man had touched her so intimately. So long since she had felt the rush of need rocketing through her that demanded satisfaction. So long since she had wanted and been wanted like this. So long.

Too long…

Still kissing her, Gavin moved a hand upward, over her rib cage, dragging his fingers lightly over each rib as he passed. Violet sucked in her breath as he pushed his hand higher, holding it when he stopped at the lower curve of her breast. She thought he would close his fingers over her completely but he surprised—and disappointed—her by pushing his hand along the line of her bra to her back. His skin was so warm through the thin fabric of her dress, spreading heat everywhere he touched her—along her spine, over her ribs again, along her shoulder blades. And then he brought his other hand into the exploration, tracing it along her torso until it rested beneath her breast...

Oh. Oh, that felt so good. Too good. So good she didn't ever want it to stop. Didn't want him to stop...

Without even realizing what she was doing, she lifted her hands to his hair and threaded her fingers through the silky tresses. It was evidently all the encouragement he needed, because he immediately deepened the kiss, thrusting his tongue into her mouth to taste her. Vaguely, she felt him draw down the zipper of her dress and unhook her bra, then she felt the heat of his bare hands splaying over her naked back.

She put up no resistance when he skimmed her dress down her torso and her bra down her arms. In response, she jerked his tie free from his collar and went to work on the buttons of his shirt, driving both hands under the soft fabric to explore what was beneath in much the same way he had her. And what was beneath was a collection of finely hewn muscle and sinew, covered by sultry, silky skin and a scattering of dark hair. His shoulders were like molten rock beneath her fingertips, his belly as hard and flat as a steam iron. And his back... Oh, his back. There seemed to be acres and acres of it, and every last inch was hot, satiny steel.

As she curled her fingers over his shoulders, Gavin dipped his head to her neck to drag his damp mouth along the tender column of her throat, then over the sensitive flesh of her shoulder. And if Violet had had any doubts before about what they were doing—and she was surprised to realize she had none—that would have made them evaporate. She wasn't sure when it had happened, this wanting him the way she did, she only knew she didn't want to fight it. When his mouth returned to hers, she kissed him with a hunger and passion that equaled, and maybe even surpassed, his own. For a long time, they only stood there half-dressed, vying for control of the embrace. Gavin tasted her deeply again and again and again, then opened to grant her the same access.

She felt his hands everywhere, pressing against her naked back, curving over her shoulders, curling around her waist, strumming up her rib cage. Then he was cradling the lower swell of her breasts in both hands, pushing upward, covering the sensitive mounds with sure fingers. When she gasped at the certainty of his possession, he plunged his tongue deeper into her mouth, palming her even more fiercely. As he kissed her and kneaded her soft flesh, it was all she could do not to buckle beneath the onslaught. She felt one hand inching down her torso, to where her dress was bunched at her waist, then felt the fabric sliding as he slowly, slowly—oh, so slowly—pushed it over her hips and legs. In response, her fingers found the button of his fly where she deftly unfastened both it and the zipper.

As Gavin guided his hands under her panties to caress her ass, she drove her fingers into his trousers, her breathing going ragged when she found him full and ready for her. He groaned when she cupped her hand over the head of his shaft and gently began to palm him, then again when she dragged her fingers along his length to its base. He stilled as she repeated the action a few more times, then gasped when she returned her attention to the tip.

And then, before she realized what was happening, he was sweeping her up into his arms and carrying her into her bedroom. The moment he set her on the floor, he began jerking at what was left of her clothing, so Violet stepped out of her shoes and aided him in the process as best she could. She shoved his shirt and jacket off his shoulders at once, and they joined her clothes on the floor. Then she skimmed her hands lightly over his chest again, caressing the dark hair that dusted his abdomen from shoulder to shoulder and from collarbone to navel, tracing the ripple of muscles beneath. He was spectacular-looking, all power and darkness and exhilaration.

"You are so beautiful."

She didn't realize it was she who had spoken aloud until she heard—and felt—the rumble of laughter bubbling deep inside his chest. When she looked up at his face, she saw him gazing at her with rabid desire, his dark hair tumbling over his forehead above tumultuous blue eyes. "No," he said softly. "*You're* beautiful."

Such a simple compliment, and an echo of one she had already paid him. But hearing Gavin say it, the way he did, made Violet feel as if she were the singularly most exquisite creature on the planet.

"What are we doing, Gavin?"

"Isn't it obvious?"

She smiled a little at that. "Okay, then maybe the question should be why are we doing this?"

He smiled, too, more confidently than she had. "Isn't it obvious?"

Instead of answering that question, she said, "I can't help thinking it's not a good idea."

"Then stop thinking, Violet. And start feeling."

And without giving her a chance to do anything else, he dipped his head to hers and kissed her again, even more hungrily than before. As Violet kissed him, she pushed at his trousers, and he helped her shed them, along with his boxers, even though she still wore her panties. When they stood together again, he covered both of her breasts with his hands, thumbing the sensitive peaks until Violet could not only not think, but could barely remember her name.

As he caressed her, he moved forward, walking her backward until the back of her thighs bumped the side of her bed. Then he turned their bodies and sat, pulling her astride him, facing him. Wrapping his arms around her waist, he moved his mouth to her breasts, first one, then the other, stroking her nipples with the flat of his tongue before drawing its tip along the lower curves. She murmured soft, satisfied sounds and threaded her fingers through his hair, desire purling through her entire body before pooling between her legs.

Then his hand was between her legs, petting her with sure fingers through the damp cotton of her panties. Violet gasped again at the intimacy of his touches, instinctively rising in his lap to escape the madness-inducing caresses. But his fingers followed, pushing hard against the fabric, finding and tracing that most sensitive part of her again and again. She cried out as ripples of pleasure wound through her, fighting the climax that began to pull at her center. Gavin seemed to sense how close she was, because he moved his hand to her thigh and gentled his mouth on her breast, barely touching her until her shudders began to subside.

Then he was turning their bodies again, until Violet lay on her back at the center of the bed, his hands going immediately to her panties. She lifted her hips so that he could pull them down, then she, too, was completely naked. For a moment, neither seemed to know what to say or do. Then Gavin covered her hand with his and guided both downward, through the soft nest of curls between her legs. He halted there and removed his hand from hers, settling it against his hip.

Confused, Violet gazed at him. But he only gazed back, seeming to think she should know what happened next.

"I don't understand," she finally said softly.

He looked at her curiously, then replied, "Touch yourself for me."

Her eyebrows shot up at that. "You want me to...?" But she couldn't quite make herself finish the question.

He nodded. "Yes. I do."

"But..."

He brought his hand back to hers and covered it again, pushing both between her legs until she could feel the wetness of her own response beneath her fingertips. Aligning his fingers with hers, he pushed her hand down deep, and heat shot through her at the contact. Then he drew her hand up again with a long, leisurely stroke... and released her. Tentatively, Violet repeated the action by herself, threading her fingers gently through the damp folds of her flesh. Without thinking about it, she cupped the other hand over her breast, catching the nipple between the V of her index and middle fingers, and pleasured herself that way, too.

The coil of heat that had begun to tense in her belly when Gavin pulled her into his lap cinched tighter still as she touched herself, multiplying when she saw the passion on Gavin's face and heard the rush of his breath as he watched her. Over and over, she stroked herself, even penetrated herself, bending her knees and bringing them to her chest to facilitate herself and titillate him. As her stroking intensified, he began to murmur hot, measured instructions for her, profane words about what she was doing to herself and what he would do to her next.

As he spoke, the waves of her climax began again, but as before, Gavin stopped her before she was lost to them. Then he rolled her onto her belly and lifted her hips so that her knees and shoulders pressed into the mattress. Vaguely, she registered the fact that he was rolling on a condom and didn't question where it had come from—a man like him would always be prepared. Then, grasping her hips in sure fingers, he knelt behind her and thrust himself easily—*deeply*—into her drenched canal from behind.

Never had she felt so full, so complete. When Gavin drove himself deeper still, Violet cried out and instinctively pushed her bottom against him. He withdrew a few scant inches, then propelled himself forward again, burying himself inside her until she wasn't sure where his body ended and hers began.

Again and again he penetrated her that way, his movements powerful, vigorous and intense. When he finally rolled her over to her back "—I want to watch your face when it happens—" he hooked her legs around his waist, and ground into her again. Violet's climax came almost immediately, with the rush of a hundred boiling oceans, wave after wave of pleasure coursing through her. But Gavin wasn't quite finished yet, and, still pounding into her, gently fingered her sensitized flesh, bringing her to a second cataclysm. She heard his voice crying out in chorus with her own, felt one final flash of utter and complete ecstasy, and then collapsed against the sweat-dampened sheet beside her.

Never in her life had she experienced the sensations and emotions Gavin had roused in her, and all she wanted in that moment of spent joy was to experience them again. Soon, she thought. Very soon. Right after she remembered who and where she was…

Eight

Gavin watched Violet sleep, his mind completely at odds with the peaceful picture that she was. Now she lay on her stomach in a shaft of ambient city light spilling from the window on the other side of the room. One hand rested on the pillow near her face, her fingers curled loosely as if she were holding on to something invisible and precious. Which, of course, she was, but Gavin didn't want to think about that right now.

The luscious, creamy expanse of her back looked silvery and otherworldly in the near-darkness, bared as it was by the sheet dipping low above her delectable derriere. A sheet, he noted, not for the first time, that was decorated with cartoon cats. Never in his life had he dated a woman who put sheets on her bed that were decorated with cartoon cats. The rest of Violet's bedroom was as quirky, a collection of flowers and fringe, beads and bangles, whorls and whimsy.

He did his best not to wake Violet as he rose, retrieving

his shorts and trousers from the floor and silently pulling on both. He shrugged into his shirt, too, but didn't bother buttoning it, then, with another glance at a still-sleeping Violet, made his way to the bedroom door. Sex always made him ravenous—especially when it was as vigorous as it had been with Violet, and especially when he'd missed a meal beforehand.

When he flicked the wall switch in her kitchen, he muttered irritably at the light that filled the minuscule room. He poked through the cabinets until he found a modest cache of sweets, which were in no way appealing. The refrigerator was a little better stocked, though the bulk of it was staples of the feminine diet—yogurt, fruit, salad stuff. He finally hit pay dirt—sort of—with a trio of cheeses in the dairy compartment. Grabbing a couple of pears, he sliced those along with the Brie, Edam and whatever the hell the other one was and placed all on an oversize plate. A basket on the counter yielded a reasonably fresh baguette for him to slice, and he found a surprisingly good, if inexpensive, pinot noir tucked behind a potted plant near the sink.

Not bad for an impromptu feast, he thought after opening that last. He gathered two wineglasses—neither of which matched the other—from one of the cabinets, then he assembled everything on a tray and headed out. His plan was to serve Violet in bed, but as he passed through the living room, his gaze lit on a candle in a ruby-red votive anchoring a stack of papers on the end table and decided it would add nicely to the arrangement on the tray.

Smiling at his own bit of whimsy, he went to retrieve it, but his hand halted just shy of closing around it. Because the papers it was sitting on were glossy pages that had been torn from a magazine, and the top one featured photographs of a very familiar sight. From a photo spread of the same that had appeared in *Chicago Homes* magazine a year and a half ago.

Gavin placed the tray of food on the coffee table and sat on the sofa, plucked the votive from the stack of papers, and began to sort through them. In addition to the *Chicago Homes* piece, there were pages torn from other magazines featuring other people's homes, along with articles about all things male-related. Or, more specifically, rich male-related. There was information on expensive clothing—including a photo from *GQ* that depicted a model wearing a twenty-five-hundred-dollar Canali suit—wool and cashmere, of course—and Santoni loafers that would set a man back at least another fifteen hundred. His tie was a silk Hermès and his shirt was a fine cotton Ferragamo.

Seeing that made him sit up a little straighter. It was the same outfit he'd read aloud about at his office, the one in chapter twenty-eight of Violet's book, where her protagonist Roxanne first met the much ballyhooed Ethan. The ensemble was almost identical to the one Gavin owned himself. Now that he thought about it, he may have even bought the pieces after reading the *GQ* article himself.

He sifted through other items about cigars, whisky and cognac that highlighted the very brands he enjoyed himself. A story about jazz music featured the very artists he most often listened to himself. There was an article about the Chicago gym where he worked out. There were reviews of restaurants where he ate and bars to which he enjoyed taking potential clients. There were stories about the exclusive men's shops where he bought his clothes and accessories. And then...

Then there was a small clipping about an exclusive, little-known shop in Alsace that made silk undergarments for men whose designs were completely unique.

He shook his head. Evidently he and Violet had both been

modeling characters after the same image. But where she had made hers completely fictional, Gavin had done his best to make his real. To make himself real. Except that, now that he thought about it, he was probably no more factual than Ethan was. He was...

Ah, hell. He was a cliché. Because of his humble beginnings, he'd had to educate himself—the same way Violet had—about what made a successful man stand out in a crowd. He still did that. He probably consulted a lot of the same sources Violet had. That was why he and Ethan had so much in common.

Good God. He really was chapter twenty-eight, Ethan. But it was he himself who had created the character, not Violet. Or, at least, he had created Ethan before she had. Strange that the two of them would think so similarly about something like that.

As he gathered up the sheaves of paper that had become scattered as he'd looked at them, he realized there was more to them than just research. There were also some printed out manuscript pages that bore signs of having been edited. Gavin smiled. Her new book. Had to be. Unable to help himself, he deftly put the pages in order and began to read.

Only to immediately wish he'd left well enough alone.

The passage started far into the book—page three hundred and fifteen—and described a confrontation between a woman who seemed to be the book's protagonist and a "character" named Mason Gavin who, it quickly became obvious, was a first-class, prime rate, see-exhibit-A SOB. On the upside, at least he was good-looking...

Mason Gavin was a real piece of work. The kind of man who could pass a homeless family in sub-zero temperatures and head into a restaurant for a hot toddy and a slab of steaming prime rib. I'd worked for a lot of egocentric, unaccommodating, chauvinist jerks in my day, but this guy... This guy was their king.

Hmm. Color him alarmist, but it didn't look like Mason Gavin was going to come out smelling like a bed of roses in this story.

He was six-feet-two and two hundred pounds of unpleasantness.

Please, Gavin thought. He was six-three and a hundred and ninety pounds. And every inch was pure muscle.

He was the sort of man who could kick a kitten to the curb, into a pile of wet slush.

Now that was just hyperbolic.

And I knew if he could do that to a kitten, he wouldn't think twice about tossing me into the company paper shredder.

He continued reading through to the last printed page, noting that Violet's editorial changes hadn't softened Mason Gavin, but had instead made him even more severe. He'd heard stories about authors who modeled characters in their novels after their enemies and then made them suffer heinous deaths, but Violet didn't seem to want death for her Mason Gavin. She merely wanted to antagonize and berate him. A lot. And she wanted her heroine to bring him down a peg or two. Or ten. When he finished the last page, he collected the rest of the scene from the cushion beside himself and began to straighten the pages. As he added them to the tidied articles, he glanced up.

Violet stood framed by the bedroom entrance, leaning against the doorjamb with her arms crossed and one foot crossed over the other.

She had gotten dressed, too—kind of—and was wearing a pair of baggy, low-riding pajama bottoms spattered with a snowflake print, topped by a snug cropped T-shirt that rode high enough to expose a delectable stretch of flesh between the two garments.

"I was kind of mad at you the day I wrote that passage," she said. "I wasn't going to keep that name for him. Wouldn't want to get sued for libel and defamation, after all."

There was something in her voice that belied her casual posture, though whether that was because she was afraid of how he was going to react to what she'd written or because she was having second thoughts about what had happened between them, he couldn't have said. Yes, she'd enjoyed their lovemaking as much as he had. But in the harsh light of waking—both literal and figurative—people often had regrets.

"What I think," he began carefully, "is that…" He sighed heavily. He held up the manuscript pages and said, "Have I really been this bad?"

She pushed herself away from the doorjamb and braved a few steps forward. "Yes," she told him, making something inside him twist painfully. Then she amended, "In the beginning, you were," and he relaxed. Some. When she took a few more steps forward, he relaxed even more. "But I guess," she continued, "in the beginning, maybe you had a reason to be."

He shook his head. "No, I didn't. I realize that now."

She smiled a little tentatively, completed the last step necessary to bring her next to the sofa, but didn't sit beside him. Instead, she gestured with her chin toward the stack of magazine pages on the end table. "I guess I could have shown you that in the beginning, so you could see how I did my research. It might have saved us both some trouble. Maybe if you could have seen then how universal a man Ethan is, and how there was nothing in my research to link him to you—"

"Except for my penthouse, you mean."

She frowned. "What are you talking about? I got Ethan's penthouse from a spread in *Chicago Homes*. I'm using it in the new book, too, because I liked it so much."

This time Gavin was the one to grin. "A spread that was done about my home."

"What?"

He sorted through the articles until he found that one. But instead of getting up from the sofa to bring it to her, he patted the cushion on the side of him in silent invitation. After only a moment's hesitation, Violet joined him. But she crowded herself deep into the corner so that a good six inches of space remained between them. He wasn't sure what that meant, after what the two of them had shared. He wasn't sure he should try to figure it out, either. One thing at a time.

"Here," he said, pointing to a line in the first paragraph. "It identifies the residence as the Chicago penthouse of CEO Gavin Mason."

Violet read the sentence he indicated, but shook her head. "I swear, I don't remember that at all. I'm not even sure I read the article. I just thumbtacked it above my desk so I could look at the pictures while I was writing."

"Well, even if you did read it, you read it a long time ago and couldn't have remembered my name. Or made the association when you learned it."

She smiled at that. It wasn't a big smile, but it wasn't

bad. "So you really do believe me," she said. "You're finally convinced you're not Ethan?"

He made a noncommittal sound at that. No need to get into that again.

"I mean, how could the book be anything but fiction, you know?" she asked further. "A woman not being taken advantage of or brutalized in the sex trade? A woman actually controlling her own sexual destiny in a male-dominated world? A woman finding sexual gratification every single time she has sex, with every single man, and never having to fake an orgasm? As if."

Gavin had started to smile, too, as she spoke, but the smile fled as she voiced that last part. "Are you saying you've faked an orgasm before?"

She bit her lower lip, a gesture that made him want to nibble it, too. "Um, yeah, Gavin. Every woman has at some point."

"Did you…tonight?" he asked, surprising himself. He'd never wondered whether or not a woman had faked it with him. And, honestly, he wasn't sure he would have cared if one had, as long as he'd found satisfaction himself. Suddenly, though, with this woman, he did care. He cared a lot.

She laughed. "You're kidding, right? How can you even ask me that?"

The relief that washed over him was almost palpable. Until he realized she hadn't actually answered the question. "So that's a no?"

"Do I have to spell it out for you?"

"Yes."

"No."

That was better.

She blushed becomingly again—he wasn't sure he would ever stop being fascinated by that—and her gaze skittered nervously away from his, falling on the papers he'd been sifting through. "So...I guess seeing all this means you're really not going to be suing me, right?"

There was still clear doubt in her voice, and he was surprised she could still ask the question. Although, after the way he'd threatened her, maybe she needed him to spell it out for her, too.

"No. I know the book is fiction. I know that I'm not Ethan. And I know that you never worked as a call girl."

She nodded at that, returned her gaze to his, and smiled. "Good." Then she sighed halfheartedly. "Now if only I could convince everyone else in the world that I'm not Roxanne," she said of her book's protagonist. "That I'm not even Raven French. I'm Violet Tandy. I'm just like everyone else." She lifted her shoulders and let them drop. "Oh, well."

Okay, that *wasn't* true. No way was Violet Tandy like everyone else. She wasn't like anyone he'd ever met before. But just who was she? And why did he suddenly want so badly to find out?

"That is going to be a problem," he said. "For both of us."

Her head reared back a bit at that. She studied him for a moment, then said, "Why would it be a problem for both of us? I mean, it's really not even that big of a problem for me. Annoying, yes, but not a problem."

He expelled a single, humorless chuckle. "Well, I can't have my friends thinking I'm dating a call girl. Especially now that it isn't true."

Her head did that rearing back thing again. She opened her mouth to reply, even inhaled a breath before speaking, then seemed to think better of whatever she had intended to say and shut it again.

"What?" he asked.

She did the open-then-close-the-mouth thing again, only

this time, she began to tap her finger restlessly atop the stack of papers, too. Finally, she said, "Um, I guess I forgot."

"Forgot what?" he asked, his confusion mounting.

She sighed heavily, and the finger began tapping even faster. "I forgot how important image is to you. Tonight… There were times at the party tonight, and here, when we…" She dropped her gaze to her lap. "You just seemed a little different tonight, that's all."

"Different from what?"

Now she looked up at him again. "Different from the guy who's so worried about what other people think of him," she said levelly. "Tonight, at least for a little while, you only seemed to care about what *I* think of you."

"I do care about that, Violet. I—"

"But you care more about what other people think, Gavin. Otherwise, it wouldn't be a problem for you that so many people still think *High Heels* is a memoir, not a novel."

He couldn't quite halt the incredulous sound that escaped him. "Oh, and I guess it doesn't bother you that so many people think you used to be a prostitute?"

"It only bothers me because it's frustrating to keep having to defend myself," she said. "Or when someone threatens to sue me."

"You honestly don't care that there are people out there saying—believing—that you used to have sex with whoever was willing to pay you the most money?"

"What other people think of me is none of my business, Gavin. Why should I waste time and energy on something like that?"

"Because image is everything."

"No, substance is everything," she immediately countered.

"No one ever gets to the substance unless they get past the image. If you don't present a flawless image, if you're not perceived as the right kind of person, you'll never get anywhere. You'll never count for anything."

She nodded at that, jerkily, angrily. "Right. Gotta have that blue-blooded pedigree to be somebody, don't you? Gotta be a part of the right society. The Gold Coast society. Can't be seen running around with riffraff like call girls and poor people."

"Violet, that wasn't what I—"

"Wasn't it? You're so worried about people finding out you started off poor and disadvantaged, not even caring that it's perfectly acceptable to have come from that—"

"There was nothing acceptable about the place I come from," he interjected coldly. "It went beyond disadvantaged. Beyond poor."

"So what?" she asked, echoing the question she'd asked that day at his office. "You're not that person anymore, Gavin. And you're never going to have to go back to that place. And even if you did end up there, it wouldn't change—"

"I will never go back there," he said vehemently. "I'll do whatever I have to do to make sure of that. And I'll do whatever I have to do to make sure not even the slightest whiff of that stink pollutes the life I have now. I don't want anything to do with the people who live in that world. People who live in that world, Violet, they're..."

He wasn't sure, but her back seemed to go up at that. Literally. "They're what?" she asked.

"They're not like you and me."

Now her chin seemed to rise a notch. "Oh, aren't they?"

"No. They don't care about anyone or anything. They're uneducated, they're lazy and they're totally content with their lousy lot in life. They don't work hard. They don't have dreams. They don't rise above. They don't count for anything in this world."

She gaped at him. "I can't believe you just said that. How can they not count for anything?"

"Because they're invisible. Nobody wants to acknowledge they exist. People like that, the rest of the world wants to sweep them under the rug or hide them behind a door."

"Then it's the rest of the world who has a problem. Not the people you grew up around. People always count for something," she stated resolutely. "Except for the ones who are mean and intolerant. Those are the ones who don't count."

Gavin said nothing in response to that. He wasn't mean or intolerant. He was simply calling it like it was.

"Maybe some of those people you knew in your old world weren't as well educated as you are now, but that doesn't mean they weren't smart. And what you saw as laziness might have been planning—or even dreaming. How do you know what goes on inside anyone's head? You're not psychic."

"You don't have to be psychic to know when people have given up."

She shook her head again. "You don't get it, do you?"

Gavin felt his own back going up now. Why was he letting her put him on the defensive when he had nothing to be defensive about? He knew what he was talking about. She didn't. He'd come from that world and knew it firsthand. She knew nothing of it. Tersely, he replied, "Get what?"

"Not everyone has to have buckets of cash to be happy," she said, with even more vehemence than before. "A lot of people find happiness wherever they can. Like in a blue, sunny sky after days of rain. Or finding out at school one day that there's going to be a surprise trip to the Field Museum, a place you've always wanted to visit but have never seen. Or having your parents stop screaming at each other long enough to hear a song you love playing on the radio. Or finding a dollar bill stuck in a street grate that you can spend any way you want, like on a Hershey bar because you never get to have those at home. In even *having* a home. A real home where you'll finally be able to—"

This time she was the one to cut herself off. She expelled an impatient sound, flexed her fingers in exasperation, then doubled them into fists again. "Guess what, Gavin? I come from exactly the same kind of world that you do. Maybe even worse."

He wasn't sure what to say to that. Not only because he couldn't imagine someone like her on the mean streets of his youth, but because, for some reason, it didn't really seem to matter where she came from. It only mattered that she was here with him now.

In spite of that, and because she seemed to need a reaction from him, he told her, "I find that hard to believe."

The response, however, only seemed to make her angrier. "Why?"

He decided to tell her the truth. "Because, Violet, you're not like anyone I've ever met before. You're not—"

"Like all those meaningless, heinous people who are born into situations they have no control over?"

"That's not—"

"You know what? You need to go."

"What?" he asked in disbelief. "Go? Why? Violet— What the hell is going on?"

"And you better hurry," she added coolly, "before any of your friends see you in this neighborhood."

"Hey, none of my friends would be caught dead in this neighborhood." Once again, he spoke without thinking, and only when the sentiment was out did he realize how callous it sounded.

Violet evidently thought so, too, because she strode straight to her bedroom, scooped up what was left of his clothing from the floor, then brought it out and threw it at him.

"Get out," she said. "And don't ever, *ever*, bother me again."

"Violet, I didn't mean—"

"Get out."

"Listen to me. I—"

"Get. Out. Now."

"But—"

"Now."

Gavin had uttered more than a few callous comments in his day, but he'd never felt obligated to apologize for any of them. He told himself he didn't have to apologize for this one, either. What he'd said may have been callous, but it wasn't untrue. Nothing of what he'd said tonight had been untrue. Besides, he hadn't reached the level of success he had by apologizing for anything. So why did he suddenly want to start now?

"You have ten seconds," she said. "Nine. Eight. Seven. Six…"

"All right," he conceded, lifting both hands, palm up, in a gesture of surrender. Funny how the night was cycling to how it had begun. Not funny, however, was the way it was now Gavin on the defensive. Not that he didn't deserve it…

But he *didn't* deserve it, he immediately told himself. He'd said nothing wrong. He knew better than Violet did what it was like to come from poverty and need. Maybe she wasn't from the blue blood, Gold Coast society he moved in now, but it was obvious she didn't know the first thing about the sort of place he'd come from. She was too unsullied for that. Too smart. Too happy. Too content.

With as much dignity as he could muster, he put on his shoes and shrugged into his jacket, stuffing his tie into a pocket with one hand as he adjusted his collar with the other.

"Look, Violet, I—"

But she ignored him, marching to the front door and jerking it open. Although it stuck in Gavin's craw to let things end this way, he knew better than to try and talk to her when she was like this. He still didn't know what he'd said or done to warrant such a reaction in her. Still didn't know what to say that might make her come around. So, for now, all he could do was exactly as she'd instructed and leave.

He felt, as much as heard, the front door slam shut behind him, then, as he was making his way down the steps, the sound of something crashing against a wall.

So what? he asked himself, voicing the very question she'd asked him. So what if he'd made her mad? So what if he'd said some unkind things about the facts of life? So what if she'd told him she never wanted to see him again?

So what if he felt like a complete SOB? He was an SOB. He'd had to be to claw his way out of his old life and carve out the one he had now. That was why no one had ever been able to bring him down.

Until this moment.

Because as Gavin descended the stairs of Violet's apartment building, he felt as though he was moving lower in other ways, too. Into shadows. Into solitude. Into cold. Into the same kind of life he'd had before. The same kind of man he'd been before. Invisible. Meaningless. Worthless.

It was the neighborhood, he told himself as he stepped out of the dilapidated building onto the crumbling front stoop and made his way down the cracked stairs. Hell, even visiting a place like this tainted his newfound way of life. The life he would protect above all else.

So Violet never wanted to see him again? Fine. He didn't want to see her, either. Not if it meant coming back to a place like this. The sooner he got home to his multi-million dollar, professionally decorated, shiningly immaculate penthouse, the better. So what if it was empty? So what if there was no one there to greet him? So what if he'd be going to bed alone? So what?

So what?

For a long time after Gavin left, Violet sat on her sofa in her pajamas, staring into her bedroom at the ten-year-old dress and cheap rhinestone jewelry scattered on the floor by the bed. What the hell had happened tonight? From the moment she had looked through the peephole to see Gavin standing on the other side of the door, nothing had made any sense. Not him coming to her apartment, not him blackmailing her into going to the party, not the fact that he had actually been nice to her—at least part of the time—not his finally realizing she wasn't who he'd thought she was after thinking otherwise for so long, and certainly not—

Not making love with him.

No, she quickly corrected herself. What they'd done hadn't had anything to do with love. Not only because they'd barely known each other a week—really, they didn't know each other at all—but because she was no more capable of feeling such an emotion than he was. What the two of them had experienced had been a simply physical reaction to…

Well, okay, she wasn't sure what it had been a reaction to. They'd obviously both been attracted to each other—for her since the moment she'd laid eyes on him. And they'd both shared some heightened emotions over the course of the week. All that anger and resentment and fear had to go somewhere once they both realized there was no reason for them to be feeling any of those things. She supposed she shouldn't be surprised that they would manifest in such raw, unbridled, steamy sex.

Sex. Not lovemaking. *Sex.*

So why did she feel so empty inside? Before, even if it wasn't good sex, Violet had always felt a little better afterward. Satisfied. Unstressed. Ready to move on to the next task, whatever it was. Sex with Gavin—and it had been *great* sex—had had the opposite effect. She felt more anxious now than she had in weeks and in no way satisfied. Instead of moving on to the next task, all she could do was replay what had happened over and over again in her head. It was going to be a long time before she could move on from this.

He thought she was nothing. That, strangely, was the thing she was having the most trouble letting go of. He'd said as much when he'd talked about his own meager background, how people from his old neighborhood had been invisible and hadn't counted for anything. He might as well have been talking about her own origins. She'd come from the same place he had. But she'd never thought anyone from that world didn't count. Especially not herself.

She wondered why she was so surprised by some of the things he'd said. She'd known how he was from the get-go. He'd said himself in his office on Monday how badly he wanted to keep everything from his old past hidden from everyone in his new life. And it wasn't as if he was alone in his opinion of poverty. There were plenty of people in the world who shared it—and most of them ran in his social circle.

What difference did it make how he felt, anyway? She'd told him she never wanted to see him again. And she didn't.

She didn't.

Really.

Even if, for one brief moment at the party, when she'd been dancing with him, he'd made her feel things she'd never felt before. Even if, while making love…ah, she meant having sex…with him, she'd felt those things again, even more strongly. The kind of things that made a person feel… close…to another person. The kind of things that made a person *want* to be close to another person.

The kind of things Violet wasn't wired to feel.

Her gaze lit on the tray of food Gavin had put together that he had obviously intended to bring to her in bed before getting sidetracked by her work. No one had ever brought her breakfast in bed. Hell, no one had ever even prepared food for her. In all her foster and group homes, that responsibility had fallen to the kids. To teach them independence, her foster parents had always said. And sometimes, they'd even meant it. Would he have prepared a romantic feast like this for her had he known who she really was and where she really came from?

She laughed humorlessly at her own question. Of course not. He wouldn't even have made love…had sex…with her tonight if he'd known that. Hell, he probably thought coming from poverty was even worse than being a call girl. At least call girls moved in high society the way he did. At least they knew how to dress and talk and behave. Call girls didn't have to rent clothing from a boutique off Michigan Avenue. They didn't have to be taught to dance. They didn't have to be given lessons about art. Gavin would be infinitely more comfortable with Raven French than he would with Violet Tandy. It was Raven he had made love…had sex… with tonight, not Violet. Had he known her true origins, he wouldn't have had anything to do with her. No way would he let the *stink* of her *pollute* the life he had now.

So why should she let the stink of him pollute hers?

She knew what she needed to do to dislodge Gavin from her brain and from her—from everything else. It took less than fifteen minutes for Violet to wash her face and brush her teeth. Then she fired up her laptop and opened the file for the novel she was writing to follow up *High Heels and Champagne and Sex, Oh, My!* She'd hit a point where she wasn't sure what to write next, had gotten bogged down in a scene where her protagonist—a naive, small-town girl who was visiting the big city for the first time—needed to fall down on her luck. Violet hadn't been sure what form, exactly, that bad luck should take.

Now she knew. Oh, boy, did she know. Mason Gavin was about to take advantage of her in a big way, then toss her to the curb along with that kitten in the icy slush.

After cracking her knuckles, she began stroking the keys slowly, ordering her thoughts as she wrote. Gradually, her typing speed increased—as did her thoughts—and she began to write in earnest.

Write what you know, she thought sardonically. *Just like Ernest Hemingway.*

Less than thirty-six hours after being tossed out of Violet's apartment, Gavin sat at his desk looking over a file that had been specially couriered to him by a private investigator he used on a regular basis. It was an interesting mix of documents and reports, all of which were related by one cohesive thread: Violet Tandy. Had he done this before Saturday night, the file would have only bolstered his certainty that she was exactly what he'd thought her initially to be: a prostitute. Because all the information in front of him indicated she'd come from exactly the kind of environment that would push a woman to become just that. An environment full of poverty and need, of loss and neglect.

She really had come from a world even worse than his own.

She was older than he'd suspected, nearly thirty, Chicago-born and -bred. After being abandoned as a young child—and he recalled now how she'd said she didn't know who her father was, a comment he'd shrugged off at the time—she'd been shuttled from one foster or group home to another. Almost a dozen by the time she turned eighteen, at which point the state had cut her loose to fend for herself, with no education, no training, no benefits, nothing. After that, with no one to rely on, she had been on her own. College had been understandably out of the question for the average student she had been in school, so she had worked at a number of menial jobs before penning her novel. As a hostess at a five-star restaurant, as a tailor's assistant at an exclusive Michigan Avenue menswear shop, in housekeeping at a luxury hotel. Places where she was exposed to the affluence of high society and the potential for her to meet rich men.

Had she wanted to become a call girl, she wouldn't have had any trouble finding clients, he was sure. Not coming from the sort of background she'd come from. Not having the access to potential clients that she'd had. Not looking the way she looked and being the way she was. No man in his right mind could have resisted her.

But she hadn't done that. She had worked honest jobs, some of them backbreaking, sometimes from sunup until sundown. She had planned. She had dreamed. And, using her wits and determination, she had pulled herself up from her meager beginnings to make those dreams a reality.

She was like him, Gavin thought. She'd started off with nothing and nobody and worked hard at whatever job she could find to survive—and succeed. She'd come up from the streets to find herself in high society. Except that where she didn't seem in any way embarrassed by her beginnings, Gavin had done whatever he could to hide his.

But then, she didn't have a business reputation or any social status to protect, did she? She didn't move in the same worlds he regularly did or have to see the same people he did every day. Her lifestyle didn't depend on keeping her origins a secret. If his colleagues and acquaintances knew the truth about him, they'd never give him the respect or friendship they gave him now. Hell, they wouldn't give him the time of day. And without professional esteem or standing in the community, Gavin might as well be right back in the gutter where he started.

No way would he let that happen.

He understood now why she had been so angry Saturday night. When he'd said people from poverty counted for nothing, she'd thought he'd been talking about her. She'd thought he meant she was nothing. That she was meaningless. That associating with someone like her would... How had he put it? Oh, yeah. Would make the stink of his old life pollute the one he had now.

With a heavy sigh, he leaned back in his big, executive chair and rested his head against its big, executive headrest. He remembered how she had talked about finding happiness in simple things and realized now that everything she'd listed had been ways she'd found happiness herself as a child. Which, he supposed, indicated she wasn't much like him, after all. Because he hadn't found happiness in anything when he was a kid.

It didn't matter, he told himself. He wouldn't be seeing her again. Even if he wanted to, she'd made clear that she didn't want him coming anywhere near her. And he shouldn't want to go near her. She was a symbol of everything he tried to keep out of his life these days. And even if she wasn't a call girl, there were plenty of people who thought she was. He had proof he could take to his friends and colleagues that indicated otherwise, and, even if he couldn't convince them the book was a work of fiction, he could eventually convince them that he wasn't Ethan.

Yeah, he'd get right on that. Enlist the help of his P.I. to gather the same information Violet had had at her apartment and get it to the proper gossipmongers in society, blah blah blah. In a few months, it would have all blown over anyway, and he'd be back in everyone's good graces. Going to all the right parties. Landing all the right clients. Dating all the right women.

Inevitably, that made him think of Violet. Who wasn't the right woman at all. Who shouldn't have mattered. Certainly no more than any other woman he had bedded, regardless of that woman's station in society. It had always been easy for Gavin to forget women. Because none of them had ever been particularly memorable. Not the one—he couldn't remember her name now—who had been the heiress to an industrial empire. Not the one whose name had started with an M, maybe an N—W?—who was a former Miss Illinois. Not the one with the red hair—or had she been a blonde?—whose ancestors had come over on the *Mayflower*. He'd forgotten them within minutes of dropping them at their front doors. Or climbing out of their beds.

So why was he still thinking about Violet? Why did he need—want—so badly to see her again?

Maybe if she understood what he had to lose, he thought. Maybe if he showed her more of his life, she would understand. She'd seen his office, but so much of what he did was off-site. And few of his real friends had been at the party Saturday night. Of course, that was because he only had a few real friends, but still. Maybe if Violet saw more of how he actually lived, she'd realize how much he had to lose and why it was so important to him to preserve that lifestyle. That was it. If she could just see what his life was really like, then she'd see why he was so adamant about protecting it. That was why he couldn't stop thinking about her. That was why he needed—wanted—so badly to see her again.

Now all he had to do was figure out how to do that without her slamming the door in his face.

Nine

A little over a week after giving Gavin the heave-ho, Violet sat in a classroom in Northwestern's castle-like University Hall, listening to one of the professors introduce her as—she tried to contain her glee—a local bestselling *novelist.* The students in the class to whom she would be speaking were studying Contemporary American *Fiction,* and she was here today to discuss literary social criticism and the ways in which *fiction* and the *novelist* reflected the society and mores of the contemporary real world.

Ah. How refreshing. There would be no questions about sex toys. No questions about lingerie. No questions about fetishes. No, Violet was here to talk about literary social criticism. So she'd rented the most conservative outfit she could find at Talk of the Town, a black Chanel suit she'd accessorized with an onyx pendant and bracelet. Her black hair was wound into a chic chignon, and she'd deliberately kept the cosmetics to a minimum. She was here to be taken seriously. She was here to be an auteur. And looking out at the fifty or so students who had come to hear her, she felt exactly like that.

She spoke at length with great confidence on her topic— she'd spent days preparing and rehearsing her talk—then opened the floor to invite questions from the students.

The first question was about sex toys.

The second question was about lingerie

The third question was about fetishes.

By the time the hour drew to a close, Violet had dropped her head into her hand and was pinching the bridge of her nose to ward off the vicious ache that had begun pounding at her forehead immediately after the question about necrophilia. With a deep, heartfelt sigh, she said, "I have time for one more question."

"What are you doing after the lecture?"

Her head snapped up at the familiar baritone, and she saw Gavin standing in the far right corner of the room, near its entrance. He must have slipped in when she had her back to the crowd, probably when she was using the dry erase board to draw her hierarchy of gender authority or her timeline of the history of pay inequity. Fat lot of good either had done. No one had even taken any notes. Not until the necrophilia question, anyway, something that gave her more than a little pause about the next generation.

She looked from Gavin to the crowd between them. More than one person seemed interested in her reply. A couple seemed *too* interested.

"Um, I have an engagement," she said. She turned quickly to the professor who had invited her to speak. "Dr. Besser, thank you so much for the opportunity to speak to your class today. It was so..." Blah blah blah blah blah.

With all the proper gratitudes and platitudes exchanged, Violet made her way to the exit that was on the other side of the lecture hall from Gavin. But he anticipated the action and doubled his speed, walking out a few seconds behind her. She managed to maintain her lead for a full five seconds before she felt his hand slip easily over her shoulder and heard his softly uttered, "Violet, please. Wait up. I need... want...to talk to you."

That odd solicitude she'd heard in his voice the night of the party was back, and, as it had that night, it melted something inside her that made her hesitate. She halted and faced him, shrugging the hand off her shoulder as she did, because it felt too good to have it there, conjuring too many memories of the night they'd spent together scarcely a week ago.

"What?" she asked, striving for petulance, but fearing she fell short, since what she actually felt was...

Well, maybe she better not try to identify that. Because whatever it was grew stronger when she looked at him. He was, as always, impeccably dressed in one of his dark power suits, this one charcoal with barely discernible pinstripes. His shirt was starched white, but his necktie was spattered with bits of blue that made his opalescent eyes look even deeper and more expressive—and sexier, dammit—than ever.

He said nothing at first, only gazed at her, scanning her features from her eyes to her mouth and back again. And looking as if maybe he were having the same kind of thoughts about her that she was about him, the kind that it was best not to think about.

Then, very softly, he said simply, "Hello."

She expelled a single, weary sigh, then, reluctantly, replied, "Hi."

Another moment passed in which the two of them only studied each other, until, finally, Violet broke the silence.

"What are you doing here, Gavin?"

"I came for you. To see you," he hastily corrected himself. Then he further amended, "I mean, I was in the area and was hoping maybe you'd have time for lunch. I have a client here," he hurried on. "He wants to sell part of his collection, so I came up to do the assessment myself. He's a very important person." That last sentence seemed tacked on, as if to answer why the CEO of the company would perform the sort of task an underling—a seriously under underling—would normally do. Which, of course, had indeed been her next question. So, she asked what she thought was another good one instead.

"How did you know I was up here?"

He looked panicky for a moment. "I saw a notice in the paper about it."

"The only notice that ran in the paper was in a special Women's Interest section that was in last weekend's edition. Call me crazy, but you don't seem like the type to read a special Women's Interest section."

Finally, he smiled, that wry, charming, confident one that did funny things to her insides. "I'll have you know I am *very* interested in women."

Even though he had obviously made the comment in jest, they both seemed to realize, as soon as he said it, that it held a lot more significance than that. Thankfully, however, he chose not to pursue the matter. Wisely, neither did Violet.

"Since my client doesn't live far from the Northwestern campus, I decided to leave a little early and see you speak."

"Why?"

His wry, charming confidence seemed to falter some. "Like I said, I need…want…to talk to you."

"Why?" she asked again.

He took his time responding, as if he wanted to rephrase whatever he had planned to say. Then he did it a second time. Then a third. "I'd like a second chance to make a first impression."

She almost laughed at that. As if a man like him could have any hope of changing a woman's memory of the first time she'd laid eyes on him. Especially since, right after laying eyes on him, he'd accused her of being a hooker. And a liar. She reminded herself not only of that, but of how he felt about people like her—people who had come from disadvantage and poverty. She reminded herself of all the things he'd said that night after the two of them made lo—ah, she meant after the two of them had sex. She was exactly the kind of person, the kind of thing, he wanted most to keep out of his life. Even if, after discovering she was the very thing he didn't want, he found it possible to overlook her past, he'd always be afraid of what his friends thought of her—and, by extension, of himself. He dated women who were like him—or, at least, what he aspired to be seen as: rich, privileged, untainted by the stink of poverty and need.

His image would *always* be more important to him than anything—anyone—else. He'd said as much himself.

"I'm not sure I have time for lunch," she lied. "I have, um, something I have to do tonight in the city." Like go home. Alone. Not that he had to know that part. Going home alone *was* something she had to do in the city. Every night. Since the one she'd spent with him. Always thinking about him and the night she'd spent with him whenever she was home alone.

"Come on," he cajoled. "Your talk began too early for you to have had time to eat anything since breakfast. I know this great Mediterranean place between here and my client's house. My treat."

How could he have known Mediterranean was her favorite fare?

"And they make a tabouli that's out of this world."

How could he have known tabouli was her favorite Mediterranean fare? He wasn't playing fair. Okay, he was playing fare. Just not fair.

Um, what was the question?

Oh, right. How about lunch?

She told herself to say no, urged herself to stand firm. Her origins made her nothing in this man's eyes. To him, she would always be sullied and unwanted. He was stone on the inside and ice on the outside, everything she wasn't, and nothing she wanted in a man. It didn't matter how hot and molten he'd made her feel when they were together, didn't matter that she'd seen a chink in his character that night at the party that suggested that, somewhere inside him, there was still a place of warmth and good humor and decency. People with convictions as strong as his didn't change. And she wasn't going to change who she was, either.

She told herself again to say no. But she heard her traitorous voice—or something—instead say, "Okay."

Violet had no idea how it happened—really, she didn't—but two hours later, she found herself sitting in the passenger seat of Gavin's plush Jaguar roadster, which was curling its way around the circular drive to the country estate of one Chatsworth Whitehall the…some Roman numeral. V maybe. She'd seen his name on the file that had been sitting in the passenger seat before she had folded herself into it. Why exactly she'd folded herself into his car was still a mystery. She'd had only one glass of wine with lunch— the tabouli really had been divine—so that couldn't have impaired her judgment.

The baklava they'd shared for dessert might have done it, though. She'd always been a sucker for baklava. And it had been while she was savoring an especially sweet mouthful that Gavin had invited her to join him on his excursion through the Whitehall estate to survey the collection his company had been hired to evaluate. The rat. She should have known better than to listen to anything anyone asked her over baklava. That was fighting dirty.

Mr. Whitehall's home…mansion…estate…enormous frigging house…looked like something out of a movie, she decided as Gavin pulled the car to a halt between a burbling fountain full of satyr statuary and a columned front porch that was roughly the size of her entire apartment. A movie about royalty. Really ancient, really powerful royalty. The building was a towering Greek Revival that reigned over acres and acres of what must have been gorgeously manicured gardens in the warmer months, complete with what appeared to be a topiary maze to one side. Violet didn't realize how rapt was her attention on the place until the passenger door opened beside her, making her flinch in surprise.

When she looked up, she saw Gavin waiting for her to emerge, his magnificent self framed by the majestic house… and looking very much like he was one with it.

He extended a hand to help her out, and, automatically, she took it. The moment her bare skin made contact with his, however, she was deluged by memories of the last time their skin had been in contact, and heat fairly swamped her. But when she tried to snatch her hand back, Gavin tightened his grip and gave her a gentle tug, pulling her to standing until their bodies were nearly flush, something else that engulfed her with memories of that night.

Instinctively, she took a step in retreat, turning toward the house instead of Gavin. But that quelled her agitation not at all. Because it only hammered home how very different the two of them were, and how very lacking she was in his eyes. She would never fit in with his kind of society. Never.

"It's spectacular, isn't it?" he said, misconstruing her reaction to the place.

She nodded silently.

"The Whitehalls have been a part of Chicago society since before the Great Fire. Since then, their fortunes have multiplied every year. After nearly a hundred and fifty years, that's a lot of multiplying."

"Yeah, no...kidding."

She was able to bite off the expletive she might have uttered otherwise. Something about a place like this made profanity seem, well, profane. Not to mention it would have made even more starkly clear the differences in her station and this one. Gavin came into contact with people and places like this all the time. Had it not been for him, Violet would never be given entrée into this world. He was comfortable among wealth like this. She was not.

He really had come a long way from the Brooklyn docks. Funny, though, she was pretty sure she'd feel right at home there.

"Chatsworth won't be here," he said, his use of his client's first name indicating they knew each other well, "but his housekeeper is expecting us."

To Violet, the word *housekeeper* conjured a woman garbed in rubber gloves and ruffled apron, armed with spray bottles, buckets and mops. But the woman who met them at the door of Chatsworth Whitehall Roman Numeral's house wore a suit even more conservative than her own, along with diamond studs and a clearly expensive gold wristwatch. She had one of those Bluetooth phones stuck in one ear and an iPad tucked under one arm. Her dark hair was pulled into a severe ponytail, and smart black glasses perched on her nose. Violet was going to go out on a limb and guess she didn't wield too many feather dusters.

"Miranda," Gavin greeted her warmly, indicating

he knew her well, too. He must get invited to play with Chatsworth on a regular basis. "It's always great to see you."

"Mr. Mason," she replied more formally. Guess she wasn't a part of the regular play group. "Mr. Whitehall has given me thorough instructions about your visit, and I've arranged for a good sampling of the pieces to be moved to the main salon for your convenience."

Main salon, Violet echoed to herself. She wondered how many more salons there were. Looking at the house again, she decided there were probably at least eighty billion.

"I've also arranged for Billings to prepare a light lunch for you and your…" For the first time, she turned to look at Violet, and Violet was immediately, irrationally, grateful for her rented designer duds. "Your…associate…" Miranda finally continued, using one of those all-inclusive, could-mean-anything identifiers, "if you didn't have a chance for lunch on your way here."

"Thank you, Miranda," Gavin said. "And thank Chatsworth and Billings, as well. But we did stop for a bite on the way."

Miranda smiled another one of those noncommittal smiles. "Excellent. This way, then."

So it was within the realm of possibility for Gavin to be considerate, Violet thought after hearing him thank even the cook…chef…meal creator to billionaires. She didn't kid herself that this was a new condition after her having scolded him that night at the party for treating the bartender so shabbily.

They followed Miranda through the massive front door and found themselves in a massive foyer, off which were a number of massive rooms collected around a massive staircase that spread up to a massive gallery on the massive second floor, all of it massively luxurious. Violet wasn't sure, but she thought even her shallow breathing echoed through the miles of open space surrounding them. It was into one of the massive rooms to the left of the staircase that Miranda led them, a space that was crowded with ornate antiques, a half-dozen marble sculptures and several paintings on easels.

"As I said, this is a sampling. The pieces Mr. Whitehall is interested in selling are tagged, and are representative of approximately two dozen others. This should give you a vague estimate of the undertaking and its value."

Vaguely, Violet was going to guess it was worth about eighty billion dollars.

"Thank you, Miranda," Gavin said. "We'll take it from here."

Oh, *we* will? Violet wanted to ask. Like she had any idea what she was doing here.

His word was evidently good enough for the housekeeper, because, with another one of her no-emotion smiles, she told Gavin to call her if he had any questions or needed any assistance. Then she was gone, leaving Violet alone with Gavin. With Gavin and eighty billion dollars' worth of art that didn't belong to either of them.

Suddenly, she was too terrified to move. What if she accidentally knocked something over? Or what if one of her buttons got caught on something? Not only would she lose her hundred-dollar damage deposit at Talk of the Town, but she'd be out eighty billion dollars more for Chatsworth's art collection.

"You don't have to be frightened, Violet," Gavin said, this time reading her reaction exactly. "Everything is insured."

Of course it was. And the deductible was probably only eighty billion dollars, so that would save her a bundle.

"I'm just going to go sit over there," she said, pointing

toward what looked like a simple, if very ornate, dining room chair. "It doesn't look that expensive."

"That chair dates back to the court of Louis the Sixteenth," Gavin told her. "It's worth more than you can imagine."

Wow. And she was someone who could imagine eighty billion dollars.

"Then I'll just stand by the door. Or maybe I should go out to the car," she further suggested.

He grinned at that. "Stick close to me. You'll be fine."

Oh, right. That was the most dangerous place of all for her to be.

In spite of that, she—very carefully—made her way to his side and stuck there like glue. In fact, to make sure she didn't accidentally bump into anything, she looped her arm through his and leaned into him. He went rigid at her action, but when she looked up at his face, his expression was anything but. He started to say something, then evidently thought better of it. Instead, with his free hand, he pulled his phone out of his pocket and began taking photos of the pieces closest to them.

That task completed, he began to take a step toward another grouping. But he didn't get far, because Violet had planted her feet too firmly in place, and he ricocheted back toward her. Instead of recoiling from him this time, however, Violet found comfort in his nearness. This place really was a little overwhelming. But somehow, for some reason, Gavin wasn't.

"It's just a house, Violet," he said quietly, again reading her correctly. "Just a house and some furniture and some things to make a place nicer, just like anyone else's."

"Oh, please," she said. "You know better than anyone that that isn't true. This house isn't like anyone else's and neither are the things in it. This is the kind of house, the kind of furniture, the kind of *world* you've always wanted desperately to be a part of and will do anything to keep living in. The one you want to preserve above all else. If this house were in my neighborhood and filled with the kind of furniture in my apartment, you wouldn't have anything to do with it."

He looked as if he were going to deny it, then must have realized she would know he was lying. "You're right," he agreed, surprising her. "But look at it, Violet." He spread his arms wide to encompass the entire room. "Look at this place. Look at these incredible things. Wouldn't you rather live someplace like this than where you're living now?"

Involuntarily—or maybe it wasn't so involuntary—she lifted her chin in defense. "I like where I'm living just fine."

"But wouldn't you rather live here?"

She surveyed her outrageously luxurious, outrageously expensive, surroundings before replying, to make sure she replied honestly. The place was gorgeous, no question. And being surrounded by such beauty and extravagance was indeed a privilege. To be here every day, knowing it all belonged to her?

She shook her head. "I don't know, Gavin. As beautiful as it all is, this is an awful lot to be responsible for. The more you have, the more you risk losing, you know?"

Instead of taking a moment to consider what she had meant to be a ponderous question, he immediately beamed at her. "Exactly. That's exactly my point."

"What is?"

"That this is so much—too much—to give up. That's why I want to protect my lifestyle. Because no one in their right mind would want to live any other way."

"No, that wasn't what I—" Then the rest of what he'd

said began to sink in. "So then, I'm not in my right mind if I prefer to live more modestly? Is that what you're saying?"

His smile fell. "No, that wasn't what I meant."

"It's what you said."

"But it's not what I meant. Violet, I've worked so hard to win cachet into society like this. It's been my dream since I was a kid. Do you know what it's like to have a dream that long? Do you know what it's like to have it come true?"

She remembered her cozy little cottage in the suburbs, with its roses and wisteria and porch swing. "I know exactly what it's like to have a dream like that," she said. She couldn't answer the second question, however. She still hadn't realized her dream. But she figured it probably felt pretty amazing to make a dream a reality. Someday, she hoped she would know for sure.

Her opinion of Gavin shifted a little with that. Maybe they weren't so different from each other at their core. They'd both come from meager beginnings and struggled for something better. Yes, his idea of *something better* was way beyond her own, but they'd still both been striving to make a dream a reality. How would Violet feel if she'd been living her ideal life in her ideal cottage, then someone came along who threatened to jeopardize it? She'd do whatever she had to protect it, the same way Gavin would.

The difference, however, was that she wouldn't walk over people to do it. She wouldn't insult them. She wouldn't tell them they didn't count. But then, that was the way it was, wasn't it? The more you had, the more you risked losing it. And the greater the risk, the greater the fight. And the greater the fight, the more ruthless the fighter.

She was glad she would never have to fight as much or as hard as he did. She was glad she would never have to pick and choose her loved ones—her friends, she hastily corrected herself—based on how much they were worth or what their origins were. She was glad she wasn't ashamed of where she came from or who she was at her core. Who she would always be, no matter what path she followed in life.

She gazed at the riches surrounding her again and decided maybe they weren't worth eighty billion dollars after all. A small cottage in the suburbs, with wisteria and roses and a wicker swing, was worth way, *way* more than all of this. And being able to fall in love with whomever you wanted, no matter where they came from or who they were or where they were going? Well, there wasn't a price that could be put on that at all. So much for Gavin's high society. So much for his success. So much for his wealth. Because if he thought living like this was what it took to be someone in the world, then he was wallowing in greater poverty now than he ever had as a kid.

Ten

Gavin sat across from Violet in the dining room of his Lakeshore Drive penthouse, watching her push her food around on her plate and avoid his gaze. He'd hoped inviting her to dinner at his place would alleviate some of the sullenness that had come over her at Chatsworth's estate, but she seemed even more subdued now than she had been then. It had taken every wheedling and cajoling gene he possessed to even get her to agree to have dinner with him. All she'd wanted after he'd concluded his business was to be taken home.

He had thought she would enjoy lunch at the restaurant he'd chosen. Not only was it was one of his favorites, it was bloody hard to win a table there, so high in demand was the place. Only the cream of society had the cachet to eat there, something he'd made sure Violet discovered via their waiter by calling ahead and promising an exorbitant tip. Gavin had thought she would enjoy the Whitehall estate even more.

Who wouldn't? It was like a museum, filled with beauty and history and riches unrivaled by any other private collection in the country. He had thought Violet would be dazzled. He had thought she would better appreciate the kind of world he lived in now versus the one he had left behind. He had thought she would begin to understand what was at stake for him, what he had to lose if he lost face with his friends and colleagues. Instead, she'd seemed kind of sad.

So he'd invited her to dinner here, thinking... Well, okay, thinking pretty much the same thing he thought when they were at the estate. That by seeing his home from something other than the pages of a magazine, she might again be better able to understand why he was so determined to protect his lifestyle. All modesty aside, his penthouse was pretty spectacular, too—maybe not Chatsworth Whitehall spectacular, but still pretty damned impressive.

It encompassed the entire top level of the high-rise and was surrounded on all sides by panoramic windows that offered magnificent views of nighttime Chicago, from the Hancock Tower to the north to Navy Pier to the south. The dining table, tucked against one such window, allowed them to see both, along with the glitter and spectacle that was the rest of Chicago, along with the black expanse of Lake Michigan, which was dotted with lights of its own thanks to the yachts and freighters making their way across the inky water. Even having lived here nearly five years, Gavin was still stunned by the beauty of it all, still had trouble believing he had risen so far from the stunted, blighted roots from which he had sprung. Why couldn't Violet be as awed by this place as he still was?

And where Chatsworth's house might have looked like a traditional art museum, Gavin's looked like one for modern art. The inner walls were dotted with twenty-first-century abstracts while a few easels scattered about held more.

His furnishings were sleek and contemporary, in muted neutrals so as not to detract from the splashes of color in the paintings.

His place was amazing, he thought, surveying it again, putting modesty aside. He had, after all, paid one of the city's top decorators a pile of money to make it that way, and one of the city's top real estate agents to find it for him. And before leaving Chatsworth's, he'd called his favorite restaurant in the city and ordered a five-star meal to be delivered a half hour after his and Violet's arrival, complete with server and cleanup crew. That, too, was a perk he enjoyed with the kind of life he led—the kind of power he wielded in both his social and professional worlds. He'd figured Violet would be as impressed by the meal as she was by her surroundings. But nothing had shaken her from her funk.

"Is it the chateaubriand?" he finally asked. "Is it under-cooked? Overcooked? Cold?"

Her head snapped up at the question, and she looked a little confused, as if she were just now remembering where she was and what she was supposed to be doing. Although he was still dressed in the suit he'd worn all day, she'd shed her ultra-conservative jacket after their arrival to reveal a shimmery top beneath that was almost the same color as her eyes. The pale amethyst against her creamy skin made him think both were made of silk, and the color only brought out even more expression and emotion in her eyes. Unfortunately, that expression wasn't delight, and the emotion wasn't happiness.

"I guess I'm not very hungry," she said halfheartedly. "That was a big lunch we had."

"Eight hours ago," he reminded her.

She lifted her shoulders and let them fall. "Slow metab-olism," she said, as if that would explain it.

Yeah, right, Gavin thought. He remembered well the night they'd spent at her apartment. Scarcely a day had gone by when he hadn't remembered it well—okay, so maybe he'd been hoping other things would happen, too, if he brought her to his place tonight. And he knew there was nothing about Violet's, ah, metabolism that could be even marginally compared to slow. Not to mention she'd been full of vitality and exuberance when she'd been speaking at Northwestern earlier in the day. Whatever had extinguished that exhilaration had happened since he had caught up with her.

"Did you not enjoy the day then?" he asked.

Another one of those tepid shrugs. "Sure. It was great."

Great, he echoed to himself. That was just...great.

He stood and moved to the other side of the table, curling his fingers over the back of her chair. Maybe he needed to point out the obvious.

"Okay, up you come," he said as he pulled her chair away from the table.

She seemed surprised by the turn of events. "What? Why?"

"If you're not hungry, then there's no point sitting here playing with your food. Come on. I'll take you on a tour of Chicago."

"Gavin, please. It's getting late. Not only do we not have time for a tour of Chicago, I grew up here, remember? I've seen everything there is to see."

He grinned and held out a hand. "Not like this, you haven't."

She expelled a weary sound and, with clear reluctance, placed her hand in his. Gavin folded his fingers over hers gently, then tugged her to standing, putting just enough effort into it to pull her body flush with his. Immediately, he dropped his hands to her hips and dipped his head to hers. But he couldn't quite bring himself to kiss her—as much as might want to.

And he did want to. Very much.

For a long moment, she only gazed at him, her fingers curled gently against his chest, as if she were making a not-very-serious attempt to keep him at bay. Her scent enveloped him, something flowery and sweet and utterly appropriate for her. Something he found very hard to resist.

Once again, he began to lower his head to hers and, for one hopeful, infinitesimal moment, she started to tip hers back for him. Then something darted across her expression, something shadowy and forlorn, and he made himself stop.

Stop and say, "To your left, we have the Hancock Tower, the tallest building in Chicago."

Violet studied him in silence for a second, then blinked a couple of times, as if she'd awakened from an enchanted slumber. "The Hancock Tower?"

He nodded, making himself pull away, and point out the window at a building in the distance that looked, in the nighttime, to be constructed of ebony and diamonds. "And over there," he said, pointing at an illuminated ribbon to the right of the Hancock Tower, "is Michigan Avenue's celebrated Miracle Mile."

Instead of looking out the window toward where he was pointing, she continued to gaze at him in confusion. So Gavin gripped her hips more resolutely and turned her entire body around, so that she was facing away from him and out at the sparkling city sprawl beyond the window. He didn't let her get far, however. In fact, when he moved to stand behind her, he made sure he was even closer than he'd been before.

He dropped his head until his mouth was right beside

her ear, then murmured softly, "And down there is Navy Pier. Surely you've visited that a time or two."

He felt, more than saw, her nod. "Only once, actually," she said softly. "When I was ten. For about three months, I lived with a couple who had taken in six of us. It was the best place I lived back then. They were genuinely good people who honestly loved the kids they cared for. They took all of us to Navy Pier one day, and we stuffed ourselves with corn dogs and cotton candy and rode all the rides."

"Even the Ferris wheel?"

She nodded again. "The Ferris wheel was my favorite."

"Then you should go back and ride it again."

Still in her dreamy voice, she said, "Yes. I should."

Very tentatively, Gavin added, "In fact, you should go back and ride it with me sometime."

Had he not been standing so close to her, he wouldn't have been able to tell she stiffened the way she did at his comment. Unmistakable, though, was the way she pulled her head to the side, away from his.

"That would work well for you, wouldn't it?" she said, her voice considerably cooler than it had been before.

Both her behavior and her question confused him. "What do you mean?"

When she turned to look at him, he saw that her sadness had fled. Unfortunately, instead of being replaced by the happiness he'd sought to instill in her, what she seemed to be feeling now was anger.

"Navy Pier would be someplace your friends would never see you with me, wouldn't it?" she said, her words clipped. "I don't imagine too many Gold Coast folks find their way to places like that. And on the Ferris wheel, it would just be the two of us. A piece of cake for you to hide me from your friends."

It was the last reaction he had expected from her. He'd spent the entire day doing exactly the opposite. Trying to invite Violet *into* his world. Trying to help her see it through his eyes. Trying to make her understand what it was like to be a part of it and why he wanted so desperately to protect his position in it.

"Violet, that's not what I—"

"Isn't it?" she asked. "Why did you drive up to Evanston today, Gavin? Really?"

There was no reason to sidestep the truth. They both already knew the answer to that. "I came to see you," he said. Hell, he'd told her that when she'd asked him the first time.

"But why Evanston?" she asked. "You could have easily picked up the phone and met me somewhere here in town."

"I didn't think you'd talk to me if I tried to call. Not after the way we—" He didn't bother to finish the statement. Neither of them could have forgotten that night. So he only said, "I'm glad you gave me a second chance today."

Her expression went dark again at that. "Yeah, well, I'd kind of hoped earlier that maybe today would be different from the last time. But it's ending exactly the same way, isn't it?"

His confusion compounded. "What do you mean?"

"That night, you made clear your disdain for people who come from the same background you do, and tonight—and today, too—you made clear you haven't changed your mind at all. You could have tried to see me anywhere in the city, but you chose to wait until I was miles away."

Because all the places in the city hadn't been the kind of places he'd wanted her to see. Not until bringing her to his place to finish the day off. "Evanston offered a good opportunity to—"

"To see me again without risk of your friends seeing me with you."

It finally dawned on him, what she was trying to say. "You think I'm ashamed to be seen with you?"

"Aren't you?"

"Of course not. I spent practically the entire day with you."

"Yeah, at places where no one you knew would be present."

"That isn't true," he said, his own defensiveness rising. "Chatsworth Whitehall is an old friend who—"

"Wasn't home," she finished for him. "And you didn't counter his housekeeper's assumption that I was one of your *associates*."

That was because he hadn't wanted to embarrass her by trying to define what her role in his life was. Not to mention he didn't exactly know what her role in his life was. He'd been hoping maybe today would make that clear. But he had no idea how to tell her that.

When he said nothing, she asked, "Why did you invite me to your place tonight?"

Gavin was really reluctant to answer that one. He would sound shallow if he told her it was because he wanted her to see what a great place he had—and, okay, maybe that was shallow, but he had hoped to make a point. And considering the direction this conversation had taken, there was no way would he would admit he'd been hoping to seduce her.

His continued lack of response, however, only seemed to make Violet more resolved that her suspicions were right. "That's what I thought. You were hoping we could repeat that night at my apartment. Then you could take me home under cover of darkness without any of your friends being the wiser that you're spending time with and sexing up someone they wouldn't approve of."

Something inside Gavin felt as if it were crumbling into bits. "Violet, we spent the entire day togeth—"

"Yeah, but we spent the day alone," she pointed out. "You might want to spend time with me, Gavin, but you don't want to do it in front of your friends. Because you know it would bring you down in their eyes."

He had no idea what to say to dissuade her of that idea. Which only cemented her belief that what she had said was true. With one final, shallow nod of her head, she strode to the sofa where she had dropped her jacket and purse and collected both. Then, without looking at him, she crossed to his front door. With a single, desolate glance at where he still stood motionless, she was gone, closing the door firmly behind herself.

By the time he found the presence of mind to follow her and jerk open the door, the elevator doors in the foyer were closing on her. The last thing he saw was the distressed expression on her face, and the last thought he had was one he didn't have time to put voice to.

What he'd wanted to tell Violet was that the two of them hadn't been alone all day because he was ashamed to be seen with her among his friends. The reason they'd been alone all day was because he would have spent the day alone anyway. The way he spent virtually every day alone. And virtually every night, too.

It dawned on him then, for the first time, that, until he met Violet, he'd been alone all the time.

Eleven

Violet paused in front of a towering creekstone Victorian mansion nestled in the heart of the Gold Coast that had been converted a half century ago from a lush millionaire's home to a private club. Gavin's private club. The kind of private club it cost more to join than Violet had made in a year at any of her previous jobs. Or at all of her previous jobs combined, for that matter. And she asked herself what she was doing here.

So what if her phone had rung within moments of her settling in the backseat of a cab after leaving his penthouse last night? So what if, when she had declined to answer it, Gavin had left a message asking—no, pleading with her—to come to his club tonight to have dinner with him? So what if tonight happened to be a night when, he'd told her, every single member of the club would be there, not to mention a host of other people who were their guests, because the mayor of Chicago would be present for a fundraiser there?

So what if this was his way of trying to prove to her that he was more than willing to be seen with her in public, amid his large circle of friends?

"Just meet me at my club," he'd begged before concluding the call the night before. "I'll call ahead and make sure you're on the list so no one will give you a problem. But please, Violet. Please come."

He'd put her on the list, she echoed to herself now, her stomach knotting. That was the condition of her being able to see him. She would have to be put on a list because she wasn't a member of the club—of the society—to which he belonged. That should be enough right there to let her know how pointless an expedition this was going to be.

She'd told herself to ignore his request and stay home. But every time she'd replayed the message—and she'd replayed it several times—there had been something in his voice she couldn't quite dismiss, something that had prevented her from giving up on him just yet. She'd finally decided that, okay, she would be there at seven. But she would be going as herself this time.

That, she had decided, would be the test. Whether or not Gavin was comfortable introducing her to his friends, with her in-your-face lack of social graces, her down-to-earth personality and her off-the-rack discount wardrobe. If he could still be his upper crusty, blue-blooded self in the face of all that, and still treat her with the respect and consideration she deserved, then maybe there was hope. Maybe.

"Ready or not, Gavin," she said to the building as she ascended the stairs, "here I come."

True to her word, she hadn't bothered renting clothes for the evening and had even eschewed the faux party clothes she had worn when Gavin had blackmailed her into going to the Steepletons' party. Instead, she'd pulled out a pair of plain black trousers and white man-style shirt that she'd had since college and paired them with black flats and simple silver hoop earrings.

Unfortunately, upon arriving at the club room he'd directed her to, she discovered she was dressed exactly like the wait staff. Gee, so maybe she belonged amid this society after all. Even if it was as a laborer.

The tuxedoed maître d' stationed at the entrance thought she was a laborer, too, because after one dismissive glance at her, he jutted a thumb to the left and barked, "Kitchen entrance is that way, honey. Show up late for your shift again, and I'll can you myself."

"I'm not an employee," she said with as much dignity as she could muster. Which, she was surprised to discover, was quite a lot. "I'm a guest."

The maître d' looked up at that, but still cast a dubious eye. "Whose guest?"

"Gavin Mason's."

Now the maître d' snapped to attention and began rifling through the papers on the host stand before him. "Yes, miss. Of course, miss. I'm sorry, miss, your name again?"

Somehow, Violet refrained from rolling her eyes. Okay, she conceded, maybe there were things she could get used to in Gavin's world. Like having people who'd treated you like carpet lint suddenly realize you have value. Of course, this guy only thought she had value for the same reason Gavin thought people had value—because she had enough money to get into a place like this—but still. It was nice to be acknowledged.

"Violet Tandy," she told the man.

It took him all of a nanosecond to find her. "Of course. Miss Tandy. Mr. Mason hasn't arrived. In fact, he called to say he hit some unexpected traffic but is on his way, and that I should show you to your table and open the Krug Grand

Cuvée that's chilling for the two of you there. Hilda," he then barked over his shoulder in the same laborer-appropriate tone he had used before. "Hilda will take your coat, Miss Tandy."

Violet had no idea what a cuvée was, but she knew *grand* was French for big, so—knowing Gavin—whatever a big cuvée was, it was bound to be expensive.

Oh, it was *champagne,* she discovered after surrendering her coat to a total stranger and following the maître d' to an intimate table for two near a crackling fireplace. And not all that big, really. Though all that gold on the label did indeed make it look very grand.

Her new best buddy opened the bottle with swift, deft artistry, but poured barely a mouthful into Violet's glass. Okay, she knew the stuff was expensive, but couldn't he do a little better than that?

"Um, could I have a little more, please?" she asked.

He looked at her as if a giant fish had just sprouted out of her forehead. "You should taste it before I pour a full glass, miss. To make sure it meets with your approval."

Oh. Faux pas number one for the evening. "Gotcha," she said, wrapping her hand around the bowl of the glass to lift it. At the maître d's discreet "Ahem," however, she looked up to find him shaking his head imperceptibly. "The stem," he whispered. "You should hold the glass by the stem, miss."

Faux pas number two, Violet thought. And Gavin hadn't even arrived yet. It was going to be a long evening. "Um, thanks," she said, genuinely grateful for the man's coaching. Obviously, he could still tell she wasn't a part of this crowd, but at least he wasn't looking down on her anymore and was trying to help her out.

She picked up the glass by its stem—score one for the laborer!—then lifted it to her mouth for a sip. Even though she wouldn't have known good champagne from bad grape juice, she nodded her approval. Mostly because, even if it was bad, it tasted very good to her.

"Lovely," she declared.

The maître d' smiled and tipped the bottle again, this time pouring a more generous portion.

"I'm sure Mr. Mason will be along any time now," he told her. "But if you need anything else, Miss Tandy, please don't hesitate to ask."

"Thanks," she told him. "I appreciate it."

"My pleasure."

Amazing how he could make that sound sincere, she thought as the maître d' strode to his post.

As she sipped her champagne and waited for Gavin, she stole a moment to take in her surroundings. Immediately, she was reminded of the Whitehall estate, because the club seemed to be striving to look like a smaller version of it. The walls were paneled in dark mahogany that had been polished to a satiny sheen, the ceiling was an ornate collection of gilded rosettes and wainscoting, and the carpet was an elegant design of jewel tones so rich and beautiful that it looked almost as if someone really had scattered rubies and emeralds and sapphires about.

The place was packed, too, with all manner of high society. A few tables away, Violet recognized the members of the group from the Gold Coast party she had attended with Gavin, the ones he'd said it was so important see the two of them together. They were as glittery and vivid as peacocks, making her feel like the same colorless mouse she had that night. So she scanned the rest of the crowd instead. But everyone there was dressed to the nines for the occasion, and all were laughing and chatting, smiling at and waving to each other as if they all knew each other well. Which they doubtless did.

And Gavin was one of them, the way he wanted most in the world to be. The way she would never be herself.

As if conjured by the thought, he appeared at the entrance to the club room, his black overcoat dotted with snowflakes, a few more melting like crystals in his dark hair. Something inside Violet melted a little then, too, just looking at him. He was so handsome. So sexy. And he had it in him to be a decent kind of guy, if only his priorities weren't so messed up. If only...

If only. The two most dangerous words in the English language. Gavin Mason was what he was. He'd been years in the making. He wasn't going to change overnight. He might never change. Certainly in a place like this, surrounded by the kind of people he strove hardest to impress, he wasn't going to be the man she needed him to be. Tonight, more than ever, he would be the unyielding aristocrat who scorned all things plebian. Like her.

Why did he still want to see her?

As if that thought, too, had conjured some kind of connection between the two of them, he glanced over at the table and saw her. Immediately, his anxious expression smoothed, and he smiled, making another chunk of ice in Violet evaporate like steam. He started to walk toward her, then the maître d' must have reminded him of his coat, too, and Gavin halted to take it off and hand it to the harried Hilda. Then he started to make his way toward Violet once more. But he was halted as soon as he stepped into the room by a couple seated near the door who beckoned to him. With an apologetic look for Violet, he moved that way to greet them. But even from where she sat, she could tell he was impatient. And something about that warmed her inside even more.

Until she felt someone staring at her. Someone who wasn't Gavin. And it was that creepy kind of staring, too, that made a person's skin prickle. When she glanced around, she saw a man leaning against a wall on the opposite side of the room amid a group of other people armed with cameras and microphones and such. Members of the media who were here to cover the event. The man was looking right at her, and when her gaze met his, he smiled at her in recognition. Creepy recognition, not wow-it's-so-great-to-see-you recognition. And she didn't recognize him at all. So she swiftly turned to see where Gavin was, and saw that he had been stopped by a second couple.

Hastily, Violet returned her attention to her champagne, enjoying a healthy quaff. Within seconds, however, the man who had been watching her was standing by the table, situating himself in such a way that she couldn't avoid looking at his crotch unless she looked up at his face. So, with a sigh of resignation, she looked up at his face. It was actually a fairly harmless-looking face, bland features beneath a crop of not-particularly-well-cut blond hair. Unlike the other men present—even the members of the media—he wore neither a tuxedo, nor a dark suit, but a pair of rumpled brown corduroys and an oatmeal-colored sweater.

"I know you," he said when her gaze connected with his. He wagged a finger at her knowingly. "You're Raven French. The author of that call girl memoir."

"It's not a memoir," Violet said wearily. "It's a novel. I'm not—"

"Yeah, whatever. I've been trying to snag an interview with you for weeks, but you never call me back. Teddy Mullins," he finally introduced himself, extending a hand to her that Violet had no desire to shake. "I write for *Chicago Fringe* magazine."

The minute she heard that, Violet knew why she hadn't returned his calls, and now she *really* didn't want to shake his hand. *Chicago Fringe* wasn't a magazine. It was the kind of publication that gave the tabloids a bad name.

"Um," she hedged now, "I'm sorry, Mr. Mullins, but all interviews have to go through my publicist at Rockcastle Books."

"The hell they do," Mullins immediately countered. "A guy at the *Sun-Times* said they didn't have any trouble at all arranging an interview."

"Through my publicist," she told him pointedly. "And that was before there was such a huge demand on my time. Now, if you'll excuse me, I'm waiting for—"

She looked for Gavin again and saw him chatting with yet another group of people. But he was gazing at her, and his expression grew concerned when he saw her talking to someone she clearly didn't want to be talking to. Immediately, he excused himself and started toward her again. But, again, he was halted by another friend.

In the meantime, Teddy Mullins pulled out the chair across from Violet and seated himself comfortably in it. Then he reached into his jacket pocket and withdrew a pen and pad of paper along with his cell phone, on which he pushed a few buttons, looked up again and said, "You don't mind if I record this interview, right?"

"Mr. Mullins," she tried again, "if you'll call my publicist at Rockcastle—her name is Marie Osterman—she can set up a time that's mutually convenient for us, and I'll be happy to talk with you then."

Key word: *mutually*. No way was she going to have time to talk that coincided with his.

"Let's just cut to the chase," was Mr. Mullins's reply.

What followed was a rapid-fire line of questioning that included more than a little profanity and rather a lot of sexual innuendo. Thankfully, he kept his voice low enough that no one at the neighboring tables could hear him. But

Violet could. And there was no way she was going to engage in any kind of dialogue. Still, she had no idea what to say or do that might shut him up. What was worse, the more she didn't answer his questions, the more they escalated to meanness and filth until he asked Violet, in the basest language known to humankind, whether or not she enjoyed having a particular body orifice penetrated during sex.

Which was right about the time Gavin showed up tableside.

And when he heard the question that Mullins had just asked, he grabbed the man by the back of his neck, jerked him out of the chair, and then shoved him hard enough to send him sprawling onto the floor.

And then he roared down at the man, "What the—" he spat out an expletive that more than rivaled Teddy's bountiful vocabulary, sounding every bit at home with it "—did you just say to her?"

Which was when every eye in the room turned to see what was happening.

"How dare you speak to her that way," Gavin continued, his voice gritty and thready and touched with a hint of an accent that was redolent of the Brooklyn docks. "Apologize to the lady. Now."

Teddy Mullins laughed at that. "Lady?" he echoed. "Dude. Do you even know who you're having dinner with here? She's a who—"

Before Teddy could even finish the ripe comment, Gavin bent down, grabbed him by his collar, pulled him to his feet, and then punched him in the jaw hard enough to send him to the floor again.

A murmur of disapproval rippled through the crowd. The women recoiled, the men shook their heads, and nobody, but nobody, came to anyone's aid. The people with whom Gavin had only moments ago been sharing pleasantries, now looked at him as if he were a complete stranger. Worse, every member of the media who had been lolling about on the other side of the room had sprung into action at the fracas and were now filming and photographing every physical blow and verbal exchange.

Twelve

Gavin seemed to realize the mood of the crowd then, Violet noted, because he glanced up from the man on the floor, whose mouth he had bloodied, at the hands he had curled into fists. With no small effort, he forced them open and looked at Violet.

At Violet. Not at the crowd. It was her reaction he was worried about. Not his friends'. Even after he did finally look around at his friends—and at the media recording his every action—it was Violet to whom he returned his attention, Violet whose response he was clearly most worried about.

Before either of them had a chance to say a word, however, Teddy Mullins was scrambling from the floor, and charging at Gavin. What followed could have been called a barroom brawl, but the fighting was too wild and unrefined to be considered such. So was the language, for that matter. The moment Teddy lunged for Gavin, Gavin turned into the streetwise bruiser he must have been in his youth, fighting as hard and as dirty as the other man, hurling epithets that would curl a dockworker's hair, his normally refined baritone moving closer and closer back to his Brooklyn roots with every passing word.

Violet stared openmouthed at the scene, having no idea what to do. Everything had happened so fast, and Gavin's response was so startling, she didn't know how to react. One minute, he had been the elegant, mannerly blueblood he enjoyed being, and the next, he was a brawler fighting for his survival.

But then she realized that wasn't it at all. He wasn't fighting for his survival. Had he been fighting for his survival, he would have been the picture of civility as he ushered Violet away from the table, then located the maître d' to politely request that Mr. Mullins be evicted from the premises forthwith. Had he been fighting for his survival, Gavin would have done anything to avoid a fight—especially a ruckus like this—because fighting was much too unseemly an activity among friends like his. And he sure as hell wouldn't have used profanity. Especially socially unacceptable profanity like that.

What he was doing was fighting for Violet. For her honor. And he didn't care that his civil, polite, socially acceptable friends saw him reverting to his street fighting ways to do it, or that the entire thing was being filmed for what would doubtless be the lead story on every eleven o'clock newscast in the city.

Mullins was on the floor again, bleeding even more than before, and Gavin was doubling his fist to hit him again, when Violet finally found the presence of mind to cry out, "Gavin, stop!"

He halted before hitting the other man again and turned to look at her.

"Stop," she said again, more softly. "He isn't worth it."

"The hell he isn't," Gavin countered. "You heard what he called you."

"It doesn't matter," she said. "He's scum. And scum doesn't count for anything in this world."

He said nothing for a moment, then nodded his head. Then he loosed Mullins's sweater and stood.

Unbelievable, Violet thought. Where Mullins was gasping for breath, Gavin was barely breathing hard. Guess you could take the boy out of the street fights, but you couldn't take the street fighter out of the boy.

Mullins, showing intelligence for the first time that evening, pushed himself up and, with one final, threatening look at Gavin, turned and made his way back to the side of the room—or beneath the trash heap…whatever—whence he had come. Gavin was bleeding, too, Violet noted, from a cut on his cheek, and his knuckles were smeared with what was either his or the other man's blood. One of his jacket sleeves was torn from the shoulder, and his necktie and collar were askew. His hair, usually so chic and flawless, stuck up on his head from where Mullins had grasped fistfuls of it during the scuffle. Gavin was oblivious to all of it. His only concern, it seemed, was Violet.

By now, everyone in the room was silent, their attention split between Gavin and Mullins—who looked ten times worse than Gavin, Violet thought, taking socially unacceptable satisfaction in the realization. The faces of the crowd, however, didn't seem to be akin to her own. Their expressions indicated their revulsion that such an ugly altercation had occurred in their rarefied midst. But Gavin didn't seem to notice any of them. He was too busy looking at Violet.

"I'm sorry," he told her.

The apology surprised her. She would have thought he would be apologizing to the crowd instead. "For what?

Defending my honor? You don't have to apologize for that."

He shook his head. "Your honor doesn't need defending. You're the most honorable person I know."

Meaning he thought she was more honorable than anyone else in the room, she thought. Something he'd just announced to the entire room. The entire room of people who, until now, he had indicated were more important than anyone else in the world.

"I'm sorry," he continued, "for not being here when that…that…" He looked over at Mullins on the other side of the room and shouted loud enough for the man—and everyone else—to hear, another ripe expletive, something that brought a collective gasp from the crowd. Which he didn't seem to notice. "…sat down. I promise you, Violet, no one like him will ever bother you again. Because anyone who tries, I'll—"

Again he raised his voice for Teddy to hear. It was thick with Brooklyn now, making the unseemly threats he called across the room sound even more menacing. Violet tried not to swoon at how well he was defending her honor. Even if the crowd did gasp even louder.

Gavin was finishing up when the maître d', who must have slipped out for a smoke during the melee, broke through the crowd and surveyed the damage.

"I'll take care of everything, Lionel," Gavin told the man before he could say a word. The Brooklyn seemed to be retreating, but it was still there. Enough to be unbelievably charming. And sexy. "Any damage to the premises, I'll cover it."

"Damage to the premises is the least of my worries, Mr. Mason," Lionel replied politely but firmly. "Nothing like this has ever happened at the club before. This is insupportable."

For the first time, Gavin seemed to realize the enormity of what had happened. He'd broken every rule he ever set for himself, had exposed himself to the elite he coveted as one of society's most common denominators. He had completely shattered everything he'd spent years building, had decimated the image he had worked so strenuously to cultivate and protect. In one rash moment, he had ceased to be Gavin Mason, VIP, and turned into some guy off the street who'd started a fight in an exclusive club and used a lot of bad words to boot.

"This is the sort of thing that could lead to revocation of membership," Lionel added.

Strangely, however, the maître d' didn't sound as if he were making a threat. He sounded as if he would regret it if something like that happened to Gavin.

Violet turned to Gavin, knowing what Lionel had suggested would be the worst kind of punishment he could sustain. Banishment. From the friends and society that meant more to him than anything, and from whom he had worked so hard for so long to keep his real self a secret.

"Well, if that's what the board decides," Gavin said, "I guess I'll just have to live with it."

Violet's mouth dropped open at that. But Gavin only smiled at her and tucked her arm through his own. "We can find our own way out, Lionel. Thanks."

She let him lead her through the club, both of them remaining silent as he collected their coats and helped her into hers before shrugging on his own. They continued in silence until they were on the street, well clear of the club. Finally, though, as if by mutual consent, they halted, just outside the milky halo of a streetlamp. The snow had lightened, but still fell in wisps of lacy white, giving the moment an otherworldly sort of feel. Or maybe it was being with Gavin that was doing that. The last several moments had taken them both beyond the worlds they'd grown accustomed to.

For a long time, he only studied her face as if seeing it for the first time. She looked at the cut on his cheek, thinking maybe she was seeing him—the real him—for the first time, too. She opened her purse and withdrew a tissue, then lifted it gently to the wound. Gavin winced a little when she touched him, but he didn't pull away.

"You're bleeding," she said unnecessarily. "We should get you to a doctor."

"It's nothing," he told her. Impatiently, he took the tissue in his own hand and shooed hers away. He patted the cut with much less care than she had shown, something that made it start bleeding harder.

"You might need stitches," she told him.

"No, I—"

He seemed to realize about the same time Violet did that they'd played out a scene similar to this one not long ago, at her apartment, with their situations reversed. But all he said was, "I don't need stitches. It's not that bad."

"You should still put something on it," she told him.

"It's not necessary."

Feeling responsible for the injury somehow, Violet said, "Look, my place is closer than yours. I have some antiseptic and Band-Aids. At least let me put something on it to be sure infection doesn't set in." And then, not quite able to help herself, she grinned. "I don't want you suing me for being the cause of some heinous wound that will leave you scarred for life. I've had enough grief from your legal department to last me a lifetime."

He made a face at that, but said nothing. Instead, he only touched the tissue to his cheek again, holding it in place this time. Violet took his free hand in hers and tugged him to the curb, then hailed a taxi parked on the opposite side. The cab ride to her place, too, was spent in silence, but neither of them released the other's hand. Violet couldn't remember the last time she'd held hands with a man. Maybe she never had. Holding hands was an affectionate gesture, something two people did when they cared about each other in a way that went beyond the sexual. She wasn't sure she had ever had a relationship like that with any member of the opposite sex. One that included both desire and affection.

She didn't ask herself why Gavin continued to hold her hand, too. Probably some misplaced leftover chivalry from the club—something about which she was still thinking and remained confused. Nevertheless, they left their fingers entwined even as they climbed the five flights of steps to her apartment. The only reason Violet finally—reluctantly—released him was because she had to retrieve her key.

Inside the apartment, she tossed her purse and coat onto the sofa, then told Gavin to follow her into the bathroom. There was barely enough room for both of them to squeeze inside, but she directed him to sit on the commode lid while she rummaged through the medicine cabinet for a half-empty tube of antibiotic cream and a wilted Band-Aid. Upon opening that last, she realized it was a pink Hello Kitty Band-Aid—well, they'd been on sale the last time she went to the grocery store—and when she held it up to show Gavin, he chuckled once and shook his head.

"That's okay. The antibiotic cream should be fine by itself," he said.

"But—"

"No, Violet," he stated decisively. "No pink Band-Aids."

She sniffed indignantly. "Fine. If you'd rather risk infection than be man enough to wear a Hello Kitty Band-Aid, it's no skin off my nose."

"Violet, no man is man enough to wear a Hello Kitty Band-Aid."

"I bet Chuck Norris is."

"I bet not."

"Fine," she repeated, a bit more petulantly. "It's stopped bleeding anyway."

She wet a clean washcloth and gently wiped away a smudge of dried blood, then dabbed a dot of antibiotic onto her fingertip. Lightly, she wiped the ointment over the wound. As she was dragging her thumb over the ridge of his cheekbone to swipe away the last of the excess, she felt his hands settle lightly on her hips, and she abruptly stilled. Her heart rate tripled at the simple touch, and her breath caught in her throat, and heat flared up from deep in her belly to warm her entire body.

"What…what are you doing?" she asked a little breathlessly.

He didn't say anything for a moment, then, very quietly, he told her, "I was beginning to get a little light-headed."

Oh, good. Then it wasn't only her.

"I just…" he continued, "I need to hold on to something for a minute. Until I get my bearings."

She dropped a hand to his hair, threading her fingers through his silky tresses. To straighten the mess Mullins had made, she told herself. That was the only reason. But he glanced up at her touch, his blue eyes looking deeper and more troubled than she'd ever seen them.

"I guess that's understandable after what happened," she said softly. "Your entire world was turned upside down tonight. That's bound to make a person feel flummoxed."

"No, that's not it," he told her. "What happened at the club tonight…" He shook his head. "I don't even want to talk about what happened at the club tonight."

No, he was probably already looking toward the future,

trying to figure out how he was going to rebuild his credibility in his social circle again.

"That isn't important," he said.

Waitaminnit. Not important? How could he say that wasn't important? It had destroyed everything he wanted most desperately to preserve.

"I want to talk about what is important, Violet," he hurried on. "It's why I invited you to the club tonight. I want to talk about us."

"Us?" she echoed, even more confused now. "But, Gavin, there is no *us.*"

He braved a small grin. "I know. That's what I want to talk about. Creating an us. I was hoping maybe you'd like to be an *us,* too. Because I'm tired of being *me.*" He lifted one shoulder and let it drop, his grin growing broader. "In more ways than one."

Now Violet smiled. "Well, you were certainly someone else tonight," she said, dropping her hands to his shoulders.

"But I was still being me."

"Yes, you were," she agreed enthusiastically. "And I very much enjoyed meeting you."

He stood, looping his arms around her waist. "Enough to want to maybe help make me an us instead of a me? I mean, it would mean you'd have to become an us instead of a me, too."

She moved her hands to his nape and wove her fingers together. "I think we can still be a couple of mes and be an us, too."

He smiled at that. "As long as we're a couple of something."

He dipped his head to hers and kissed her lightly, gently, almost as if he were sealing a pact with her. But then, she was kind of sealing a pact with him, too.

"You really did mess up your social standing tonight, you know," she said. "You might never be able to come back from a scene like that."

"Sure, I will," he told her.

"How? Because you have as much money as them?"

He smiled again. "Sweetheart, I have way more money than them. But that's not how."

"Then how?"

"I'll do it by association."

She nodded at that, a small thread of disappointment winding through her. She supposed he would never reach a point where he wasn't convinced that, in order to be respected, he had to move in the right social circles.

"By associating," he said, "with the most amazing, most wonderful, most sought-after woman in town."

The thread of disappointment suddenly unraveled. When he put it that way...

"I'm sorry for the things I said about..." He sighed. "About people like us. I'm sorry I was so narrow-minded and so bigoted and so...wrong. There's a lot to be said for coming from the wrong part of town. For one thing, it allows you to know what's really important."

"Money and social standing?" she asked, fully aware he knew better than that.

He shook his head. "People who care about you for who you really are, in spite of everything else. People you can care about in return, in the very same way."

"So you're saying you care about me, Gavin?" she asked, already knowing the answer to that, too.

"No, Violet. I'm saying I love you."

The warmth inside her spread like a conflagration at that. "I love you, too."

He pulled her close and kissed her again, a long, steady, deep-throated kiss that promised much more later.

"You know, in spite of everything," he said as he pulled back, "I confess that, even when I was threatening to sue you, part of me wouldn't have minded being chapter twenty-eight in your book."

"Oh, really?"

"In fact, I have to confess that, even now, there's still a part of me that wouldn't mind being chapter twenty-eight. Not being Roxanne's—or even Raven French's—chapter twenty-eight. But maybe being Violet Tandy's chapter twenty-eight."

He brushed his lips lightly over her temple, and something buzzed hard in her belly.

"Or," he continued softly, "even Violet Tandy's chapters one through twenty-seven."

Now he dragged his mouth lightly over her cheek.

"And her prologue."

A kiss to her jaw.

"And her table of contents."

A kiss to her nose.

"All her indices and appendices."

Now he moved his mouth to the sensitive column of her throat.

"All her citations."

Kiss.

"Her foreword and afterword."

Kiss. Kiss.

"Her headers and footers."

Kiss. Kiss. Kiss.

"Hell, I wouldn't even mind being her epilogue."

By now, Violet's pulse was raging faster and hotter than a nuclear warhead. "But being my epilogue," she managed to say breathlessly, "would mean being with me at the very end of my story. That you'd be my happily ever after. And that I'd be yours."

"Well, if you must…"

He leaned toward her again, pressing his mouth to her neck once more, and covering her breast completely with his hand. She gasped at the forwardness and immediacy of the intimate contact, but lifted her hands to his hair again, threading them through the thick mass to pull his head closer still.

"Which means," he murmured against her throat as he massaged her tender flesh, "that it's time to get started on chapter twenty-nine."

She pressed her mouth to his temple this time, then dragged it down along his jaw, covering his mouth with hers hungrily, needfully, passionately. "Don't you want to eat something first?" she asked as she tore her lips from his. "I mean, we missed dinner."

"Oh, believe me, I plan to eat something." He moved his mouth to her ear and told her exactly what was on his menu in earthy—and in no uncertain—terms. Then he carried her back into her bedroom so they could get right to work on their next chapter.

To say nothing of their happy ending.

Epilogue

Violet nestled more deeply into her pillow, savoring the softness of the vanilla-scented sheets and the thrum of a purr near her ear. Desdemona, the one-eyed Siamese cat she'd rescued from the Evanston animal shelter where she volunteered three days a week, made it a habit to curl herself around Violet's head when she slept, while three-legged Edgar and schizophrenic Pippin, the two tabbies, snored happily at the foot of the bed. Norton the asthmatic Basset hound huffed on the floor beside the bed, where the blind Greyhound Betsy whined good-naturedly by his side. It was a chorus to which Violet awoke every morning, and to her, it was the most beautiful symphony in the world.

Warm sunlight filtered through the lace curtains that covered the window above the bed, but she didn't want to open her eyes just yet. It was Sunday morning, the one day of the week when she could sleep as late as she wanted. And with Gavin lying in bed beside her—nuzzling her from head to toe—as he had been on so many mornings lately, it was a safe bet she wouldn't be getting up any time soon. Even in his sleep, his arm was roped across her waist and his head was bent to hers. She could scarcely believe eight months had passed since he'd stormed into her book signing in the city. In some ways, it felt as if no time at all had passed. In other ways...

Well. In other ways, she felt as if it had been a lifetime since last October.

What a difference eight months could make. When she had met Gavin, the weather had been cold and bitter, the unforgiving wind whipping off Lake Superior like an angry CEO hell-bent on suing someone he wrongly thought was defaming him. But now, on the cusp of July, the days and nights were mild enough to sleep with the windows open. Ten months ago, she'd had to walk up five flights of steps to reach her tiny urban apartment. But thanks to the combination of book advances and royalties—not to mention a movie option on *High Heels*—Violet had been able to make a down-payment on a snug little cottage in Evanston.

A cottage that had white clapboard and black shutters and a picket fence encircling its front yard. One where wisteria and morning glory grew lush and fragrant beneath their canopy of sugar maple and oak. One whose kitchen was so often filled with the aroma of cheerful pastries. One with a white wicker swing on the front porch where Violet both read and wrote during the day, and where she and Gavin spent lazy evenings counting fireflies and stars.

Who would have ever thought a man like him could engage in such pointless, whimsical activities? But then, she thought further, there had been times when she was a kid when she wouldn't have thought she would enjoy such things, either.

She'd spent virtually her entire life planning this little house in the 'burbs. She'd designed it down to the last cobblestone in the garden. And now it was hers. The only dream she'd ever dared to dream in her life had actually come true.

Okay, the only dream she'd ever dared to dream when she was a child. There was another dream she'd begun to entertain fairly recently—about eight months ago, in fact— that she would love to see come true, too. But unlike the house in the 'burbs, that dream wasn't entirely up to her to see fulfilled. Oh, she could do her best on her part, but when a dream included someone other than oneself—especially when that someone else was a man like Gavin—there was only so much one could do to make it come true.

As if she'd spoken the thought aloud, Gavin stirred in his sleep, the arm on her waist flexing, the legs entwined with hers curling inward to bring her closer. Violet loved those few moments when he was between sleep and consciousness, because he was so relaxed and peaceful, so much more himself than he was during the workday. Although, she had to admit, even the CEO Gavin had mellowed considerably since last fall. It had taken months for the gossip about his altercation with Mullins to quiet down, but he had been bothered by none of it.

In fact, when his adversaries in the business world heard about it, Gavin had suddenly found himself with far fewer adversaries in the business world. And he would be featured in next month's issue of *Fortune* magazine with an article about how a savvy kid from the Brooklyn docks had parlayed his street-smarts, integrity and grit into a multi-billion-dollar corporation.

In fact, his social status had been elevated in a lot of ways once people found out about his origins. People called him more admirable, more likeable, more *real* than he'd been before. The same had held true for Violet, once it became more obvious to the public at large that she wasn't Raven French, or Roxanne, or anyone else fictional. And, too, she'd discovered that being the author of pot-boiling bestsellers had its own sort of cachet that allowed her to move freely in society. She was as sought-after a party guest as Gavin was. In fact, the two of them together had become quite the power couple on the Gold Coast scene.

The two of them together, she echoed to herself. There was her dream again. Funny how much it had been popping into her head the past few weeks.

Gavin's hand splayed open over her belly, and he sighed softly by her ear, bringing her thoughts out of the future and back to the present—for now. He nuzzled her hair and kissed her ear, then rolled her onto her back to face him.

"Good morning," he said, his voice low and sleep-husky.

"It is a good morning, isn't it?"

He smiled and dipped his head, brushing his lips lightly over hers. "Any morning waking up next to you is a good morning," he told her.

She smiled back. "Then you've been having a lot of good mornings lately."

"Yes, I have."

Because they had been waking up together a lot lately, either here in her house or at Gavin's condo in town. It hadn't always been that way. At first, they'd danced around the overnight thing and had only spent entire nights together when they'd gone out somewhere and stayed too late to make separate trips home convenient. Since Violet had bought the house, however, overnights had become more commonplace, and almost always happened here. It was as if her act of home ownership had sparked something in both of them that drove them closer together. Toward her lifestyle, though. Not his.

That was probably significant, she thought, not for the first time. But she was afraid to think too much further than that.

Gavin levered himself up on one elbow, propping his head in one hand. "So, what do you want to do today?"

Violet thought for a moment, then said, "Nothing. In fact, I want to spend the entire week doing nothing." She eyed him thoughtfully. "Can you take the week off so you can do nothing with me?"

He shook his head. "'Fraid not. We have a major collection coming in from Italy this week, and I need to be involved. But why do you want to do nothing this week? You have a book coming out on Tuesday."

"That's exactly why I want to do nothing," she told him. "I have a tradition of hiding out for the entirety of the week whenever I have a book out."

"How can that be a tradition?" he asked. "Before this one, you'd only ever had one book published."

"Yeah, but I hid out the first week of sale for *High Heels* because I was so wigged out by the thought of having a book out there in the world, and look how well it sold. Coincidence? I think not. Therefore, I have to make sure that, for the rest of my life, whenever I have a book out, I need to disappear for the first week of sale." She thought for a moment. "And I also need to wear red socks the first day of sale, since I wore red socks the first day of sale for *High Heels*." She thought some more. "And also eat beef Stroganoff for dinner that day, since that was what I ate for dinner the first day of sale for *High Heels*."

He was grinning at her again. "Is that all?"

"Let me think." She did for a few minutes more, then ticked off the other things she remembered doing the first week of sale for *High Heels,* including getting her hair cut at Misha's Salon in Wicker Park, buying organic mangoes at Earth Star Foods, going to the Field Museum and renting a nice outfit from Talk of the Town off Michigan Avenue.

"You don't have to rent clothes anymore," Gavin pointed out when she was finished. "You're the author of pot-boiling bestsellers making money hand over fist."

"Doesn't matter," she told him. "I have to make sure I do everything the same way every time a new book comes out in order to ensure its success. Including hiding out."

He shook his head at that. "You're a terrible business-woman, you know that? You're supposed to get out there as soon as a book hits the shelves and get in some face time. Glad-hand the booksellers and jobbers and autograph the stock. Make sure they have your backlist on shelves with the new title and have you face-out on an endcap. You can't do any of that if you're hiding out."

"Signing stock?" she echoed, grinning. "Jobbers? Back-list? Face out? Endcap? That's writerspeak. Where did you hear all that?"

He shrugged, but there was something a little self-conscious in the gesture. "I've been doing some research. Reading articles and checking out some websites."

Her grin broadened. "And why would you do that?"

"I figure you did a lot of research on me and my work life when you wrote that first book, even if it was inadvertent. I need to be as well informed about you and yours."

"Why?" she asked playfully. "Are you planning to write a book about me?"

He shook his head. "No. You planning to write one about me?"

"Not a chance. I'm not sharing you with anybody, ever again."

She hadn't meant to speak that frankly. Even after eight

months of exclusivity, neither of them had ever talked about exclusivity. Neither had discussed plans for the future. Yes, Violet loved Gavin, and she'd grown accustomed enough to the feeling that it no longer frightened her. Losing Gavin was scary, not loving him. But in eight months, she hadn't really even feared that.

Until now.

Because now she had let slip something that, if he paid too close attention, would let him know how she felt. How much he'd come to mean to her. How much he'd become a part of her life. How she couldn't envision living that life without him.

So she hurried on, "Besides, I'm nearly finished with the new book, and there's no room in it for a grumpy, if disarmingly handsome, curmudgeon." She deliberately miscast him in such a way—he hadn't been grumpy for months—in the hopes that he would seize on that for objection and completely not hear the part about her not sharing him with anyone, ever again.

He eyed her warily for a moment, and in that moment, she held her breath. *Grumpy curmudgeon,* she willed him to say. *Forget about…that other thing I said.*

But he said nothing at all, only watched her silently some more.

Grumpy curmudgeon, she thought again. *Grumpy. Curmudgeon.*

Her thoughts strayed off, however, as she gazed at him. The shadows of the lace curtains dappled sunlight on his broad shoulders and mingled with the dark hair scattered across his brawny chest. They'd spent enough time on the beach this summer that a luscious, dusky bronze limned every elegant camber of muscle. His dark hair was rumpled from both sleep and their lovemaking, a thick shaft spilling onto his forehead over eyes made even bluer by the cornflower-spattered sheets. Only a man completely confident of his masculinity could look so...so...so... She bit back an involuntary sigh that erupted from a hot place deep in the pit of her belly. So incredibly *manly*...tangled up in flowered sheets the way Gavin was.

Still studying her intently, he finally said, very quietly, "You don't want to share me with anyone? Not ever again?"

Damn. So much for grumpy curmudgeon.

She made herself be honest. "No. I don't."

She held her breath again as she waited to see how he would reply. There was another long silence punctuated by his intense scrutiny. Then, slowly, he smiled. "Good. I don't want to share you with anyone ever again, either."

Something in Violet took flight at that. "Really?"

"That can't come as a surprise to you. Can it?"

Really, she supposed it didn't. Still, she felt incredibly lucky at the moment. There was something about having one's hopes confirmed that made a person feel lighter than air. "No, I don't guess it does. It's just strange to actually talk about..."

"What?" he asked when she trailed off without finishing.

She expelled a restless sound. "About...the future," she finally said. "A future that includes something besides this house. I've never really thought about a future beyond that. About a future with..." She smiled. "With someone else in it."

He smiled back. "Well, do you realize that if we start mentioning this future together in public, it could make people talk. You know how Chicagoans love to gossip. Especially the social circles we travel in."

"I do," she said. "But there's a way to get around that."

"Oh?"

"Yeah. Move away from Chicago."

He arched his dark eyebrows at that. "You trying to get rid of me now? I thought we had a future together."

"I didn't say that," she told him. "I meant you could live somewhere outside Chicago. Somewhere like... Oh, I don't know... Here."

"Here in Evanston?"

"Here in this house. With me."

Wow. She really hadn't planned to put that out there like that. Not so soon, even if they were talking about the future. Still, now that it *was* out there, she kind of liked the way it sounded. She hoped Gavin would, too. A cozy cottage in the 'burbs wasn't exactly his idea of high society. What would his friends say about such small square footage?

He said nothing for a moment, and, for a moment, she feared maybe she *had* said too much too soon, or that some small part of him did still care about what people said. Then he lifted a hand to her hair and tucked an errant strand behind one ear very affectionately. "There's another way to deal with the gossip, you know. In addition to my moving in here with you," he hastened to add.

The thing that had taken flight in Violet absolutely soared at that. "Is there?"

He nodded. "You could marry me and make an honest man out of me. That would show them."

Heat splashed into her belly at that, and the soaring thing entered the stratosphere. "You...you want to get married?" she asked softly, a little incredulously.

He grinned. "Well, since you're proposing anyway, sure."

Gee, so much for doing nothing today. Not to mention doing everything exactly the same way for her new book's on-sale week as she'd done for the last one. Getting engaged kinda threw a wrench into all that.

But as thrown wrenches went, that was a really good one.

Her silence must have given Gavin the impression that she wasn't as keen on the idea as he was, because his smile fell, and uncertainty clouded his eyes. "I mean…" he stammered, "I thought… That is…" He swallowed visibly. "We don't have to talk about this right now if you don't want to."

"No, I want to," she hurried to assure him. "I just…I'm not sure what to say."

"You could start by saying you want to get married. To me."

"I want to get married. To you."

His entire body seemed to relax at that. "Good. Then I don't think there's a lot more we have to talk about. We're getting married. I'm going to move in with you here." His smile returned, full force. "And they lived happily ever after. The end."

"You can't end it there!" she exclaimed. "That's too abrupt. The reader would be left feeling cheated."

"Well, what else does a reader need besides a happy ending?"

What indeed? Violet thought. "Well, when you put it that way…"

Gavin cupped his hand lightly over her shoulder, then brushed his fingers slowly down the length of her arm, over her wrist, her hand, her fingertips, under the sheet to settle gently on the curve of her hip. "I suppose we could give the reader one more love scene," he said softly.

She lifted a hand to brush back an especially unruly lock of hair that had fallen over his forehead. "I told you. I don't want to share you anymore. Not even with my readers."

His hand fell from her hip to her belly, then traveled up her torso to cover one breast. "Then maybe we should give them one of those behind closed doors things."

Violet skimmed her fingertips over his cheek, along the

strong line of his jaw, over his finely sculpted lips. Along his throat, over his collarbone, tracing the very, very enticing line of hair that went from his chest to the narrow of his waist. "Behind closed doors would be good," she said. "Even if the door isn't exactly closed."

He lowered his head to hers. "I was speaking figuratively."

"I wish you'd stop speaking altogether."

"Actions speak louder than words, is that it?"

"Show, don't tell."

Because Gavin had said everything that needed to be said. Now all that was left was for them to get on with it. With their actions. With their life. With their love.

Oh, wait, she realized belatedly. There was one thing left to say.

"I love you, Gavin. With all my heart."

He grinned at that. "I love you, Violet. With all my soul."

And really, when all was said—and done, though they'd be doing some, ah, doing here soon, too—that was all either of them needed for a happily-ever-after-the-end.

* * * * *

COMING NEXT MONTH

Available March 8, 2011

#2071 HIS HEIR, HER HONOR
Catherine Mann
Rich, Rugged & Royal

#2072 REVEALED: HIS SECRET CHILD
Sandra Hyatt
The Takeover

#2073 BILLIONAIRE BABY DILEMMA
Barbara Dunlop
Billionaires and Babies

#2074 SEDUCING HIS OPPOSITION
Katherine Garbera
Miami Nights

#2075 ONE NIGHT WITH PRINCE CHARMING
Anna DePalo

#2076 PROMOTED TO WIFE?
Paula Roe

REQUEST YOUR FREE BOOKS!

2 FREE NOVELS
PLUS 2
FREE GIFTS!

Silhouette®

Desire®

Passionate, Powerful, Provocative!

YES! Please send me 2 FREE Silhouette Desire® novels and my 2 FREE gifts (gifts are worth about $10). After receiving them, if I don't wish to receive any more books, I can return the shipping statement marked "cancel." If I don't cancel, I will receive 6 brand-new novels every month and be billed just $4.05 per book in the U.S. or $4.74 per book in Canada. That's a saving of at least 15% off the cover price! It's quite a bargain! Shipping and handling is just 50¢ per book in the U.S. and 75¢ per book in Canada.* I understand that accepting the 2 free books and gifts places me under no obligation to buy anything. I can always return a shipment and cancel at any time. Even if I never buy another book, the two free books and gifts are mine to keep forever.

225/326 SDN FC65

Name _____ (PLEASE PRINT)

Address _____ Apt. #

City _____ State/Prov. _____ Zip/Postal Code

Signature (if under 18, a parent or guardian must sign)

Mail to the **Reader Service**:

IN U.S.A.: P.O. Box 1867, Buffalo, NY 14240-1867
IN CANADA: P.O. Box 609, Fort Erie, Ontario L2A 5X3

Not valid for current subscribers to Silhouette Desire books.

Want to try two free books from another line?
Call 1-800-873-8635 or visit www.ReaderService.com.

* Terms and prices subject to change without notice. Prices do not include applicable taxes. Sales tax applicable in N.Y. Canadian residents will be charged applicable taxes. Offer not valid in Quebec. This offer is limited to one order per household. All orders subject to credit approval. Credit or debit balances in a customer's account(s) may be offset by any other outstanding balance owed by or to the customer. Please allow 4 to 6 weeks for delivery. Offer available while quantities last.

Your Privacy—The Reader Service is committed to protecting your privacy. Our Privacy Policy is available online at www.ReaderService.com or upon request from the Reader Service.

We make a portion of our mailing list available to reputable third parties that offer products we believe may interest you. If you prefer that we not exchange your name with third parties, or if you wish to clarify or modify your communication preferences, please visit us at www.ReaderService.com/consumerchoice or write to us at Reader Service Preference Service, P.O. Box 9062, Buffalo, NY 14269. Include your complete name and address.

SDES11

USA TODAY *bestselling author Lynne Graham*
is back with a thrilling new trilogy
SECRETLY PREGNANT, CONVENIENTLY WED

Three heroines must marry alpha males to keep
their dreams...but Alejandro, Angelo and Cesario
are not about to be tamed!

Book 1—JEMIMA'S SECRET
Available March 2011 from Harlequin Presents®.

JEMIMA yanked open a drawer in the sideboard to find
Alfie's birth certificate. Her son was her husband's child.
It was a question of telling the truth whether she liked it or
not. She extended the certificate to Alejandro.

"This has to be nonsense," Alejandro asserted.

"Well, if you can find some other way of explaining how
I managed to give birth by that date and Alfie not be yours,
I'd like to hear it," Jemima challenged.

Alejandro glanced up, golden eyes bright as blades and
as dangerous. "All this proves is that you must still have
been pregnant when you walked out on our marriage. It
does not automatically follow that the child is mine."

"'I know it doesn't suit you to hear this news now and I
really didn't want to tell you. But I can't lie to you about it.
Someday Alfie may want to look you up and get acquainted."

"If what you have just told me is the truth, if that little
boy does prove to be mine, it was vindictive and extremely
selfish of you to leave me in ignorance!"

Jemima paled. "When I left you, I had no idea that I was
still pregnant."

"Two years is a long period of time, yet you made no
attempt to inform me that I might be a father. I will want
DNA tests to confirm your claim before I make any deci-

sion about what I want to do."

"Do as you like," she told him curtly. "*I* know who Alfie's father is and there has never been any doubt of his identity."

"I will make arrangements for the tests to be carried out and I will see you again when the result is available," Alejandro drawled with lashings of dark Spanish masculine reserve.

"I'll contact a solicitor and start the divorce," Jemima proffered in turn.

Alejandro's eyes narrowed in a piercing scrutiny that made her uncomfortable. "It would be foolish to do anything before we have that DNA result."

"I disagree," Jemima flashed back. "I should have applied for a divorce the minute I left you!"

Alejandro quirked an ebony brow. "And why didn't you?"

Jemima dealt him a fulminating glance but said nothing, merely moving past him to open her front door in a blunt invitation for him to leave.

"I'll be in touch," he delivered on the doorstep.

What is Alejandro's next move? Perhaps rekindling their marriage is the only solution! But will Jemima agree?

*Find out in Lynne Graham's
exciting new romance
JEMIMA'S SECRET*

*Available March 2011
from Harlequin Presents®.*

HPEXP0311

Start your Best Body today with these top 3 nutrition tips!

1. SHOP THE PERIMETER OF THE GROCERY STORE: The good stuff—fruits, veggies, lean proteins and dairy—always line the outer edges of the store. When you veer into the center aisles, you enter the temptation zone, where the unhealthy foods live.

2. WATCH PORTION SIZES: Most portion sizes in restaurants are nearly twice the size of a true serving and at home, it's easy to "clean your plate." Use these easy serving guidelines:
- Protein: the palm of your hand
- Grains or Fruit: a cup of your hand
- Veggies: the palm of two open hands

3. USE THE RAINBOW RULE FOR PRODUCE: Your produce drawers should be filled with every color of fruits and vegetables. The greater the variety, the more vitamins and other nutrients you add to your diet.

Find these and many more helpful tips in

YOUR BEST BODY NOW
by
TOSCA RENO
WITH STACY BAKER

Bestselling Author of
THE EAT-CLEAN DIET

Available wherever books are sold!

SAME GREAT STORIES AND AUTHORS!

Starting April 2011,
Silhouette Desire will become
Harlequin Desire, but rest assured
that this series will continue to be
the ultimate destination for Powerful,
Passionate and Provocative Romance
with the same great authors that
you've come to know and love!

❖ Harlequin®

Desire

ALWAYS POWERFUL, PASSIONATE
AND PROVOCATIVE